THE CHIEFTAIN WITHOUT A HEART

Dutton books by Barbara Cartland

Love Locked In
The Wild, Unwilling Wife
Love, Lords, and Lady-Birds
The Passion and the Flower
The Ghost Who Fell in Love
I Seek the Miraculous

Barbara Cartland

THE CHIEFTAIN WITHOUT A HEART

E.P. DUTTON
New York

For information contact: E.P. Dutton, 2 Park Avenue, New York, N.Y. 10016

Library of Congress Cataloging in Publication Data

Cartland, Barbara, 1905-
The chieftain without a heart.

I. Title.
PZ3.C247Ch 1978 [PR6005.A765] 813'.5'4 77-28876

ISBN: 0-525-07985-8

Published simultaneously in Canada by Clarke, Irwin & Company Limited, Toronto and Vancouver

10 9 8 7 6 5 4 3 2 1

First Edition

Author's Note

The word "tartan" is derived from the French *tertaine,* and the first written reference to Highland dress occurs in the "Saga of Magnus Barefoot" in 1093.

In 1538 James V ordered himself the first Highland suit ever worn by a member of the Royal Family. Until the nineteenth century it was the custom of the women of the house to weave whatever tartan was required by the family.

When the Dress Act of 1746 made it illegal for Highlanders to wear a kilt or a tartan, to play the pipes or to carry arms in place of swords, they carried sticks, and, as a substitute for the dirk, a shorter knife was adopted, called a "skean dhu." This was small enough to be concealed in a pocket or stuck in the top of a stocking.

When in 1822 King George IV decided to visit his mother's Kingdom, a journey no crowned King had made since Charles I, he wore full Highland regalia, the Royal Stewart tartan.

All the details of his Reception and engagements in Edinburgh are correct and come from *A Historical Account of His Majesty's Visit to Scotland,* published in 1822.

THE CHIEFTAIN WITHOUT A HEART

Chapter One

1822

"Thank God we are in calm waters!"

Lord Hinchley poured himself a glass of brandy and drank it in one draught.

"You have been fortunate," his companion replied. "I have known the sea to be far worse than it has been on this voyage."

"Then the Lord knows that I will not come to this outlandish spot again! As it is, I am fully prepared to believe it is the Devil's country, peopled only by barbarians!"

"A popular English misconception about Scotland!" the Duke of Strathnarn said cynically.

Lord Hinchley threw himself down in a chair which was no longer swinging from side to side in the comfortable Saloon of the ship in which they had been buffeted about in an unpleasantly rough North Sea for the last seven days.

"If you ask me," he said confidentially, "you were extremely wise when you shook the soil of Scotland from your feet and came South. You have made a mistake, as I have told you before, Taran, in returning."

The Duke's face darkened and he went to the porthole to stare out at the tree-covered land past which the ship was sailing on its way up the Firth of Tay.

He had no intention of explaining, even to his closest friend, that every instinct in his body rebelled at the thought of coming back to the land he had left in a fury twelve years earlier.

He had been only sixteen at the time, and the cruelty of his father, which had not only bruised his body but humiliated his pride, had made him swear that for the rest of his life he would never have anything to do with Scotland or its people.

He remembered how he had crept aboard the first available ship in Perth harbour, and, unable to afford more than the poorest passage, had suffered intolerably in the airless, stinking hold below decks.

But his late mother's relatives in London had welcomed him with open arms.

They had sent him to a famous Public School and afterwards to Oxford University; and as the Marquis of Narn, sponsored by his grandfather who had been in attendance on the Prince Regent, he had found life both civilised and enjoyable.

He had in fact almost forgotten that Scotland even existed.

When his grandfather died he left him a large estate and a great deal of money. Basking in the friendship of the Regent, who by now was King George IV, he found in London everything he wanted and everything he enjoyed.

It had come like a bomb-shell three months ago to hear that his father was dead and he was now not only the Duke of Strathnarn but also Chieftain of the Clan McNarn.

Somehow he had always believed his father to be indestructible.

When he thought of him, which was seldom, he

had seemed ageless and terrifying, like one of the ancient giants described in the ballads sung by the Bard which he had listened to when he was a child.

He was silent for so long that Lord Hinchley, rising to pour himself another brandy, said:

"You look depressed, Taran, and that glowering expression on your face is grim enough to frighten your Clansmen, or whatever you call them."

"And a good thing if they are frightened," the Duke replied, "because in that case they are more likely to obey me."

Even as he spoke he knew he was libelling the McNarns, for the Clansmen invariably obeyed their Chiefs. In fact, he remembered his father saying once:

"A Chief stands halfway between his own people and God."

Then he told himself almost by way of reassurance that the days of such servitude were over, and now that a Chief no longer had the power of life and death over his people their feelings for him would obviously not be the same.

"Well, all I can say," Lord Hinchley remarked as he sipped his brandy, "is that if I have to travel back in the *Royal George* with His Majesty I shall lie down in my cabin and drink myself insensible until we reach Tilbury."

"It will be calmer on your return," the Duke said automatically, as if he was thinking of something else, "and as the King is a good sailor he will expect you to be on your feet, telling him how much the Scots appreciated his visit."

"The question is—will they?" Lord Hinchley asked. "I blame Walter Scott for inspiring the Monarch with this urgent desire to come to Edinburgh. If the Scots have any sense they will cut him down with their claymores and stick their dirks into him!"

The Duke did not speak and Lord Hinchley continued:

"My grandfather served in the Cumberland Army which took part in the Battle of Culloden. His description of the manner in which the Scots were massacred and the cruelties inflicted on the survivors afterwards should make any Englishman think twice before he braves the vengeance which is undoubtedly still seething in their breasts."

"It was a long time ago," the Duke remarked.

"I would not mind betting you they have not forgotten," Lord Hinchley replied.

"I think you are right about that."

"Of course I am right!" Lord Hinchley said positively. "All barbaric people have their feuds, their vendettas, their curses, which are carried on from generation to generation."

"You are very voluble on the subject," the Duke remarked.

"When His Majesty told me I was to come here as an advance guard and see that he was properly received when he arrives in Edinburgh, I took the trouble to mug up some of the facts about Scotland and the Scots."

Lord Hinchley paused before he added:

"I do not mind telling you, Taran, that the English behaved damned badly to the wretched people they conquered, entirely because they were better organised and carried muskets."

The Duke did not reply and after a moment Lord Hinchley said:

"My grandfather used to relate to me when I was a small boy how the Clans were mowed down at Culloden as they marched, hungry and wet after a night in the open, across a bad terrain, their Chiefs leading them straight into the gun-fire."

The Duke rose to his feet with what was an angry gesture.

"For God's sake, William, stop trying to make my flesh creep about battles that happened long before we were born. We have both been pressured into coming on this cursed voyage and the quicker we do what we have to do and return home the better!"

There was so much anger in the Duke's voice that his friend looked at him curiously. Then he said:

"I had the idea that this, in fact, is your home."

He saw the Duke's fingers clench as if he had touched him on the raw. Then because he was extremely fond of his friend he said in a soothing tone:

"Have another drink. There is nothing like good French brandy to make the world seem a pleasanter place."

The Duke filled his glass from the crystal decanter, which had a broad flat bottom so that it would not fall off the table with the roll of the ship.

As he felt the fiery liquid seeping through his body, he knew that instead of soothing him and bringing him some comfort it merely accentuated his anger and apprehension at what lay ahead.

He had had no intention when his father died of returning to Scotland. He had cut himself off from the McNarns when he had run away with his back crossed and bleeding from the weals inflicted by his father's whip.

If they liked to think of him as a renegade they could do so. He did not intend to concern himself with anyone's feelings but his own.

After he left University he had found that with plenty of money to spend, and with looks which made women gravitate towards him like moths to a lighted candle, he had no time to think of anything but his own pleasure.

The Prince Regent liked to have young Bucks and

Beaux round him, encouraging them in the extravagances of dress that he affected himself.

It was a fashion that had been set by his friend Beau Brummell, to which he still adhered even after they had quarrelled and Brummell had died in exile.

It was with the keen excitement of a child going to his first party that the King was planning now to appear in Scotland in full Highland regalia.

He had ordered those who were to be in attendance on him in Edinburgh to wear their tartans and finally to lead their Clans at an enormous review that was to take place on the Portobello Sands on Friday, August 23.

The Duke had not thought for a moment that he would be expected to be present, but the King had made it quite clear that he must be there, and although he wished to refuse he had found it impossible to find a plausible excuse.

But His Majesty's command, for it was little else, only came after he was in fact already considering whether or not he should return to Scotland, having received an urgent request to do so from his Comptroller, Mr. Robert Dunblane.

The communication had been brought to him as speedily as possible, though that meant that even by sea it had taken an inordinately long time for it to reach him.

Robert Dunblane had been Comptroller to his father, and the Duke remembered him as being almost the only human person to whom he could talk when he was a boy.

It was Dunblane who had informed him three months earlier of his father's death and had made it clear in his letter that he assumed the Duke would be coming to Scotland as soon as it was possible.

The Duke had read the letter and tossed it to one side.

His Clan, his Castle, and the land he owned could rot as far as he was concerned!

He was prepared to use the title that was now his, but otherwise the less he heard of the North the better, and he had in fact dismissed Robert Dunblane's letter from his mind.

The second letter was different and not only his eyes but his whole expression darkened as he read what it contained.

Finally he swore aloud:

"Fool! That damned young fool! How could he do anything so crazy?"

He could only remember his nephew, Torquil McNarn, as a crying baby who had been born in 1806, four years before he left home, but he remembered his sister Janet with nothing but love and affection.

She had been much older than he and had taken the place of his mother, who had died when he was very young.

She had married a cousin, also by the name of McNarn, and had unfortunately left the Castle and him to the merciless tyranny of their father.

The only happy memories the Duke had of Scotland were of Janet, and when six years ago she too had died he thought his last link had been severed forever with those whom he was forced, however much he loathed them, to call his kith and kin.

Robert Dunblane's letter had aroused, even if reluctantly, a sense of responsibility towards Janet's son and had made it quite clear to the Duke what he was expected to do.

"Torquil McNarn is not only Your Grace's nephew," he had written, "but also the *Dighre* [heir] both to the title and your position as Chief until you have a son."

The Duke had forgotten that Scottish inheritance could be in the female as well as in the male line.

He found himself wondering what Janet's son was like and if in fact he would make a better Chieftain of the Clan than he was himself.

Then he told himself cynically that if the boy was counting on that it would be a mistake. He supposed that sooner or later he would marry, although he had no inclination to do so at the moment.

There were too many alluring women to keep him amused when he was not involved with sport for him to think it necessary to choose one as a permanent companion.

He was convinced that if he did so he would soon find her a dead bore.

Women were amusing, the Duke had found, as long as they were elusive, as long as they could be pursued and hunted as if they were an animal or a bird, or a trophy to be won.

As soon as they were conquered and there was no more mystery about them, both his interest and his desire faded.

Then he was off again after another prey, and there was, in his opinion, nothing more time-wasting than a love-affair which had lost its dash and its spirit.

Even the King had remonstrated with him over what the women he left broken-hearted called his "callousness and cruelty."

"What is the matter with you, Taran?" His Majesty asked. "You have more love-affairs in a year than I have horses in my stable."

"Like you, Sire, I am looking for a winner," the Duke had replied.

The King had chuckled, admitting that he himself was invariably beguiled by a new and pretty face.

"At the same time, Taran," he went on, "you must remember that these frail creatures have feelings, and in my opinion you leave too many of them weeping."

"A woman only weeps when she cannot get what she

wants," the Duke replied cynically. "They must learn to accept the inevitable, Sire: I am unobtainable."

The King had laughed, but nevertheless the Duke had been scowling when he had related the story to his friend William.

"What does he expect me to do?" he had asked. "Marry every woman to whom I make love?"

"No, of course not," Lord Hinchley replied, "but you are savage with them, Taran. Surely one of them must touch your heart?"

"I have no heart," the Duke said positively.

Lord Hinchley smiled.

"That is a challenge to Fate. One day you will fall in love, and then you will understand how agonising it can be to see someone you adore looking over your shoulder to find someone better than yourself."

The Duke smiled cynically, and his friend exclaimed:

"Dammit, Taran, you are too conceited. You are thinking that it is an impossibility because you are the best. All right, go on until retribution catches up with you!"

"And if it does, which is very unlikely," the Duke replied, "I shall still have had a good run for my money!"

Lord Hinchley broke in on the Duke's thoughts now by asking:

"What happens when we arrive?"

"I have not the slightest idea," the Duke replied. "I sent word to my Comptroller telling him the name of the ship on which we are sailing and the approximate date on which we should dock in Perth. I presume he will make arrangements to convey us to the Castle. If not, you may have to walk!"

Lord Hinchley gave a groan of anguish and the Duke said:

"It is no more than twenty miles! But the mountains

are very steep for those who are not used to them."

"I know you are roasting me," Lord Hinchley said. "At the same time, in this benighted land fiction might become an unpleasant fact. For God's sake, Taran, let us hope for the best even if we have to expect the worst."

The Duke, however, was pleasantly surprised when after the ship had docked Robert Dunblane came on board.

A tall, good-looking man of over fifty, he certainly looked impressive in a kilt, his bonnet on the side of his greying head and a plaid clasped with a huge cairngorm brooch over his shoulder.

The Duke held out his hand.

"I should have known you anywhere, Dunblane!"

"Unfortunately, Your Grace, I cannot return the compliment," Robert Dunblane replied.

There was however a smile on his lips which told the Duke that he was delighted by his appearance.

It must certainly have been hard for him to recognise the thin boy with wild, defiant eyes, whom he had last seen fighting back his tears, in the tall, incredibly handsome man of the world who now stood in front of him.

The tight-fitting hose-pipe pantaloons, the cut-away coat with its long tails, and the crisp whiteness of an intricately tied cravat did nothing to detract from the Duke's broad shoulders and his athletic figure, tapering down to narrow hips.

Robert Dunblane also noted the McNarn characteristics: the straight, aristocratic nose and the firm, authoritative mouth which could set in a sharp line.

"I suppose," the Duke said after the first courteous pleasantries had been exchanged, "that you have some way of conveying Lord Hinchley and me to the Castle?"

Robert Dunblane smiled.

"There are horses, Your Grace, waiting for you,

or, if you prefer, a carriage. But may I suggest, in case you have forgotten, that the roads are very dusty at this time of the year and by far the quickest way is as the crow flies across the moors."

"Then we will ride," the Duke said. "If that suits you, William?"

"I am prepared to accept any mode of travel," Lord Hinchley replied, "except that which involves me in going by sea!"

"You have had a rough journey, My Lord?" Robert Dunblane asked solicitously.

"Damnably rough!" Lord Hinchley replied. "If I had not been able to drown my sorrows in the traditional manner I should have undoubtedly ended up in a watery grave!"

The Duke laughed.

"His Lordship exaggerates!" he said. "It was rather choppy at times, but fortunately the wind was behind us—otherwise it might have been far worse!"

"Impossible!" Lord Hinchley exclaimed, and they all laughed.

It was a sunny day with enough wind to sweep the midges away as they set off on the horses which Mr. Dunblane had provided for them.

Leaving the "Fair City" of Perth, they travelled North, passing the Royal Palace of Scone where the Duke remembered many Coronations had taken place.

He wondered if Lord Hinchley would be interested in knowing that Parliaments and General Councils had been convened at Scone between the accession of Alexander I, who had been born in 1078 and the death of Robert III in 1406.

But he told himself with a wry smile that the English were not impressed by Scottish history and had done their best to stamp out anything that appertained to the prestige or importance of what was to all intents and purposes a conquered Colony.

Then he realised with a start that he was thinking of himself as Scottish and resenting perhaps for the first time in years the English habit of disparaging the Scots and looking on them as uncouth savages.

He believed that a great deal of their hostility and indifference as well as their cruelty was due to fear.

There was some reason for this, for it was only thirty years ago that the troops at Register House in Edinburgh, inflamed by seditious propaganda, had shouted: "Damn the King!"

He remembered too that throughout the country when the news arrived of the victories of the French under Napoleon, the Scots had planted green fir trees, symbolic of liberty.

But this was over now. George IV was coming to Scotland and everyone had been told it was a gesture of friendship.

"I do not know whether His Grace has told you," Lord Hinchley was saying to Robert Dunblane as they rode along, "but I have to leave for Edinburgh in a day or so to prepare for His Majesty's visit."

"I imagine, My Lord, you would prefer to go by road," Mr. Dunblane replied.

"Most certainly!" Lord Hinchley answered. "I shall not be able to look at the sea for a long time without a shudder."

"I hope one of His Grace's carriages will prove more comfortable," Mr. Dunblane said courteously.

The Duke was thinking that if his friend had any sense he would ride.

It was very pleasant to feel a horse between his knees as they climbed above the city with its wide silver river to see the moors purple with heather and above them far in the distance the great heights of the Grampian Mountains.

Silhouetted against the sky, with small pockets of

snow still dazzlingly white against their peaks, they were very beautiful.

A covey of grouse rose at the Duke's feet, the old cock with its warning "caw-caw" swinging them away to safety in the valley.

They were climbing all the time until finally at the top of the moor Mr. Dunblane drew his horse to a standstill and they knew that he wanted them to look back at the magnificent vista that lay behind them.

The Firth was a brilliant blue in the sunshine, the spires and roofs of Perth sprawled beside the river, and there was in the wildness of the heather a feeling of freedom.

Surveying it, the Duke felt as if he had escaped from the confines of what had been almost like prison, and it was a sensation for which he could not find an explanation.

He was remembering the expressions on the faces of the servants who had been waiting for them when they left the ship.

Mr. Dunblane had introduced to him the man who was in charge, a huge, rough Scot whose eyes when they met the Duke's had an expression of devotion that was inescapable.

'After all these years, can I still mean something to those who bear the same name as myself?' the Duke wondered to himself.

He would have liked to question Robert Dunblane about it but told himself he would feel embarrassed because Lord Hinchley would undoubtedly laugh at his curiosity.

He recalled how vehemently he had complained about coming on the journey in the first place and how often he had reiterated how much he hated Scotland.

"If you hate it so much, why are you going back?" William Hinchley had asked one evening at dinner.

"Family reasons," the Duke replied briefly.

Because he knew it would be intruding on his privacy, Lord Hinchley had not questioned his friend further.

He had, however, thought to himself that Taran was a strangely unpredictable creature.

He had a warm affection for him and it was impossible not to admire him as a sportsman, but at the same time he thought there were deep reserves in the Scot which he had found in no other man of his acquaintance.

He had thought, as they were close friends, that there would be nothing they could not discuss, nothing which would be a "taboo" subject.

And yet he found that where the McNarns were concerned the Duke was not prepared to talk.

Now, riding across the top of the moors, they could move more swiftly and found as they descended a hill that the horses achieved quite a considerable pace.

Both the Duke and Lord Hinchley were used to spending long hours in the saddle. They also drove to Newmarket Races without finding it fatiguing, and they had raced against each other and the King's record often enough to Brighton.

Yet Lord Hinchley was in fact relieved when two hours later Mr. Dunblane said:

"We have only a short distance to go now and we shall see the Castle in five minutes."

The Duke had seen it often enough in boyhood, and yet when they rounded a crag and saw it ahead it was impossible not to feel that it was larger, more impressive, and more overpowering even than he remembered.

A great grey stone edifice of towers and turrets, with ancient arrow-slits and seventeenth-century additions, Narn Castle was one of the most outstanding and certainly the most magnificent of the Castles in the whole of the Highlands.

Lord Hinchley gasped and stared at it with undisguised admiration.

"Good God, Taran!" he said. "You never told me that you owned anything as fine as, if not finer than, Windsor Castle!"

"I am glad it impresses you," the Duke said dryly.

He could not, however, help a faint stirring of pride within himself.

He had hated the Castle. It had stood like a dark shadow across his childhood, to become so menacing, so oppressive, that when he had fled from it in the middle of the night he never thought that he would go back.

Yet, with the sunshine on its windows, with its flag flying in the breeze above the highest tower, with its command over the surrounding countryside, he knew it was a fitting background for the Chief of the McNarns.

He glanced back to see if the grooms who had been following them were still in sight.

The luggage was to travel by road, but they had also been escorted by six men on horse-back and now the Duke realised they were drawing closer and not keeping their distance as they had during the long ride.

He turned his head to go forward again and Robert Dunblane said quietly:

"They will be waiting outside the Castle to greet Your Grace."

"They?" the Duke questioned. "Who?"

"The Clansmen. Only those of course who live in the immediate neighbourhood. The others will be coming in from the hills tomorrow or the day after."

The Duke was silent for a moment, then he asked:

"What for?"

It was a sharp question and he knew there was a touch of apprehension in it.

Mr. Dunblane glanced at him swiftly from under his dark eye-brows.

"To welcome a new Chieftain there is always a traditional ceremonial and they have been waiting eagerly for your return."

The Duke did not reply.

It was impossible for him to say to Mr. Dunblane that until his second letter he had had no intention of returning.

Vaguely he remembered his father holding meetings of the Clan, to which he had not been invited, and festivities at Christmas, to which he had.

Now he was recalling how important a Chief was to his people, and though he had reassured himself in London that such things were out-of-date he knew that he had been mistaken.

He wished he had made it clear to Dunblane in the letter which announced his arrival that he wanted no fuss, no special greetings, no Clansmen paying him homage.

Then he thought that even if he had said so, it was very unlikely that anyone would have paid any attention.

A Chieftain was the father of his Clan, and as previously he had had the right of life and death over his people he had been equally responsible for their welfare.

What was it he had read in some book when he had been at Oxford? It had been explaining the position of the Chieftains before the Rebellions in 1715 and 1745 and stated:

As landlord, father-figure, judge, and general, his power was great and absolute, but on occasions he would debate major issues with the members of his family and leading members of his Clan.

One thing was quite certain, the Duke thought sharply—he had no immediate family or plans to debate.

His father was dead, thank God, and so unfortunately was his sister Janet.

That left Torquil, and it was that foolish young man, his heir presumptive, who had brought him back to Scotland from the comfort and the amusements of London.

And yet he supposed there were other relatives, whom he had not remembered, and in a voice deliberately casual he asked Robert Dunblane:

"Is there anyone staying at the Castle?"

"Only Jamie, Your Grace,"

The Duke looked puzzled.

"Jamie?"

"Lady Janet's younger son."

"Of course!"

The Duke remembered now, but he had not recalled the name.

It was due to her second son that she had died in childbirth.

"He is a very amusing little boy," Mr. Dunblane was saying. "Brave, adventurous, and a true McNarn in every way."

"Being adventurous is not a quality I am particularly looking for in my nephews at the moment!" the Duke said shortly.

It was a rebuke and Mr. Dunblane looked anxious for a moment, but he said nothing.

Then, so unexpectedly that it made both Lord Hinchley and the Duke start, men appeared from the concealment of the heather and came hurrying round them.

Their arms were raised in greeting and at the same time their mouths opened to give a war-like cry which the Duke recognised as the slogan of the McNarns.

It was a wild, savage exaltation, either as a reminder of the heroic past or as an invitation to slaughter the enemy.

The Duke remembered that it was part of the Clan's identity, as was the badge of heather, gale, ling, or myrtle, which the men wore in their bonnets.

The slogan was yelled and yelled again. Then there was the high sweet note of the pipes and the Clansmen fell in beside the horses and marched with them towards the Castle.

Almost before he was aware of it the Duke found himself riding alone ahead, while Mr. Dunblane and Lord Hinchley rode behind him, with the escort of six horsemen which had joined them.

It was a procession, and a moment later the noise of the pipes was drowned with a cry from hundreds of throats and he saw the Clansmen waiting for him along the drive that led to the Castle.

They looked strange, rough, and poor, yet there was a pride in their bearing, a width to their shoulders, and a strength to their arms which told the Duke that they were men to be reckoned with.

The uproar was tremendous and there was no question of his speaking to any individual or making any response, except a gesture with his hand and a bow of his head.

Then as he reached the Castle door the noise and the voices ceased suddenly, as did the music of the pipes.

The Clansmen watched him in silence and as they clustered round him the Duke could see their wives and children beyond them, taking no part, but peeping from behind the shrubs and over the brow of the heather.

He had meant to walk straight into the Castle, but something stronger than his own desire, some instinct to do what was right, which he could not ignore, made him stand facing the men who had welcomed him.

"Thank you," he said in a voice that carried. "Thank you, and may good fortune attend us all."

It was a greeting which came to his mind from the past, but the strange thing was that he had said it in Gaelic, the language he had not spoken or thought of for twelve years!

As a great cheer went up, spontaneous and whole-hearted, the Duke raised his arm as if in salute and, turning, walked into the Castle.

* * *

"Now tell me what my nephew has done," the Duke said.

They had finished dinner and Lord Hinchley had retired to another room while the Duke had taken Dunblane into the Library, where his father had always sat.

As he crossed the threshold his eyes expected to see the dark shadow of the man he had always hated at the desk by the window which overlooked the Glen below.

The Duke had always thought his father was like a gargoyle staring balefully and menacingly out over the land he owned.

Strangely enough, the room was far from the dark cavern of misery and despair that he remembered.

The magnificently appointed Library had been designed by William Adam with a symmetry and a beauty that was indescribable.

The Duke stood looking round him, thinking it was impossible that the room had been like this when he was a boy and he had not realised its perfection.

Now the colourful leather-bound books seemed to exude a benign influence and the shadow of his father receded.

Without really thinking about it, the Duke sat down automatically in the chair his father had always occupied and invited Dunblane to sit opposite him.

"I gathered from your letter that the situation is desperate, but I can hardly believe that to be the truth," the Duke went on.

"It is certainly very serious, Your Grace."

"In what way?"

"Torquil is a prisoner of the Kilcraigs."

"A prisoner? Surely they cannot intend to incarcerate him in a dungeon or lock him up in a cellar indefinitely?"

The Duke spoke lightly.

"I imagine his quarters, whatever they may be, are none too comfortable," Mr. Dunblane replied, "but the alternative, I understand, is to send him to Edinburgh to stand trial."

"To stand trial?"

There was no doubt that the Duke was startled. "On what charge?"

"The charge of cattle-stealing, Your Grace!"

"Good God!"

There was no doubt now that the Duke was astonished.

"I have seen The Kilcraig, Your Grace, and he informs me that, while he will wait to discuss it with you on your arrival, there is no doubt in his mind that Torquil and his associates, if they are taken before the Justices, will be severely punished—in fact very likely transported!"

The Duke was stunned into silence.

He was well aware that cattle-stealing was frowned upon by the authorities and very severe sentences were passed on those who committed such crimes.

The growth of the beef trade in the Lowlands and in England had increased cattle-thieving and what was known as "blackmail." The levying of blackmail was an old Border and Highland custom.

"Mails" were the rents paid in money and in kind on Scottish estates, and "blackmail" was the tribute paid by law-abiding men to freebooters or raiding Clansmen in return for a promise that their stock would not be lifted or their steadings burnt.

Offenders were no longer hanged as had been usual in the past, but the Justices had no compunction in transporting a convicted man to the Colonies or sending him to prison for a long sentence.

"Why the devil did you allow the boy to do anything so inane?" the Duke asked angrily.

Mr. Dunblane sighed.

"I had discussed Torquil's position with your father for many years, Your Grace. I told him that he had not enough to do, and, as was inevitable, he got into mischief."

Mr. Dunblane's voice had a pleading note in it as he went on:

"I believe, quite frankly, that it was just a boyish prank. The Kilcraigs have always been our avowed enemies, and it amused him to slip across the border at night to steal away a calf or, if possible, a prime animal and bring it home in triumph."

The Duke could understand all too clearly what Mr. Dunblane was saying. It would have been a triumph because the McNarns through age-long feuds had always hated the Kilcraigs, just as the Kilcraigs hated the McNarns.

They had warred between themselves for as long as anyone could remember, and the fact that the Kilcraigs had herds of good cattle would be an enticement in itself.

Aloud the Duke asked briefly:

"How was he caught?"

"Apparently it is not the first time he has played this sort of prank," Mr. Dunblane replied, "although unfortunately I had not heard of it until The Kilcraig informed me that Torquil and the three boys with him had been taken prisoner."

"The herdsmen had lain in wait for them, I suppose?"

Mr. Dunblane nodded.

"I imagine," the Duke went on, "that they were foolish enough to go by the same route to the same place as they had done before."

"It was the nearest to the border," Mr. Dunblane said briefly.

"I cannot imagine anything more irresponsible or more infuriating!" the Duke exclaimed. "I suppose The Kilcraig will see reason if I talk to him?"

"He said he would negotiate with no-one but yourself, Your Grace."

The Duke sighed.

"Then I suppose I shall have to see him. I do not mind telling you, Dunblane, that I am extremely angry about the whole thing."

"I was afraid you would be, Your Grace. At the same time, it would have been reasonable to send Torquil to school and later to a University."

"But my father would not listen to reason," the Duke said cynically. "How old is Torquil now?"

"He will be seventeen on his next birthday, Your Grace—he is the same age as you were when you ran away."

The information, the Duke knew, was given to make him realise that Torquil had felt just as he himself had: rebellious, angry, and determined to do something about it.

"Has he been educated at all?" he asked.

"Yes, Your Grace. Your father engaged several

excellent Tutors for him, but unfortunately he found them boring."

"I am not surprised at that," the Duke said, "knowing the type of men my father would engage."

"He needs, Your Grace, to play games with boys of his own age and his own class."

"And those who were captured with him?"

"Crofters' sons, decent boys, but of course, Your Grace, uneducated."

"The whole thing is out-of-date! Ridiculous! It should never have been allowed to happen!" the Duke stormed.

Even as he spoke he knew that he was being unfair.

Dunblane had surely done the best he could for Torquil, just as he had done the best he could for himself; but, against his father's obstinacy and supreme authority, anything he could have suggested would have proved hopeless from the start.

"Well, what are we going to do?" he asked more quietly.

"I have arranged tentatively for you to call and see The Kilcraig tomorrow. He will not come here."

"Do you mean that I have to go to him?"

"It may seem a loss of face. At the same time, he holds the trump card, Your Grace."

"Torquil!" the Duke murmured.

"Exactly!"

"Very well. But I warn you, Dunblane, that if The Kilcraig makes it too difficult I shall tell young Torquil he can go to the Devil!"

The Duke spoke violently, but even as he did so he knew he was shadow-boxing.

It would be quite impossible for him to allow his nephew and heir presumptive to go up for trial in the Edinburgh Courts like a common felon.

What was more, it would not be Torquil who would be humiliated and punished, but the whole Clan.

They all bore the same name, and they all believed themselves to be part of the same stock.

He knew that every Clansman on his lands would fight to the death for his own family and his honour, just as he would fight any battle into which his Chief might lead him.

"The sooner we get this over the better!" the Duke said sharply. "Send a message to The Kilcraig that I will call on him at noon tomorrow. I presume you will come with me?"

"If you are going into Kilcraig country, Your Grace, you must travel as befits your position. Not to do so would be looked upon as a sign of weakness."

The Duke looked at his Comptroller in surprise.

"What does that imply?"

"You will go with your immediate henchmen, Bard, Piper, and gillies, as your forefathers travelled before you."

"God in Heaven! In this day and age, is this necessary?" the Duke asked.

"As I have said already, if you do anything else it will be looked on as a sign of weakness, and at the moment, as Your Grace knows full well, you have no good cards in your hand."

The Duke thumped his clenched fist on the arm of his chair.

"This is intolerable! What is more, I feel, Dunblane, as if I have stepped back into the past. In England, noblemen do not hold each other's children as prisoners. Duelling is almost out-of-date, and arguments are conducted in a gentlemanly manner over a glass of port!"

"Unfortunately, Your Grace, The Kilcraig is very like your father, who would always rather have used a claymore than had a sensible argument."

"Very well," the Duke said harshly. "Have it your own way! I will leave everything to you, Dunblane, and I only hope we can retain some vestige of pride out of all this tomfoolery!"

He walked towards the door, and only as he reached it did he turn back to say:

"Do you expect me to get myself up in fancy-dress?"

"If you mean should you wear the tartan, Your Grace, you must meet The Kilcraig as a Chieftain—the Chief of the McNarns."

The Duke did not reply but went out of the Library, slamming the door behind him.

Chapter Two

The Duke was in an extremely bad temper.

He had in fact got up with what his Highland Nurse would have called "a wee black devil" on his shoulder.

His valet had laid out for him, obviously on Mr. Dunblane's instructions, the Highland dress that he had brought from London.

He had taken very little interest in it and had merely given the order to his tailor to make what was necessary.

He was to realise later that the tailor was in fact a conscientious man who had taken immense trouble in finding out what was the correct regalia for a Chieftain.

After he had finished his bath, the Duke saw lying on the chair trews of skin-tight tartan, which a Chief would wear when he preferred to ride rather than walk.

There was also a tartan jacket, a tartan waist-coat, and the plaid that would be clasped with a silver-and-cairngorm brooch on his left shoulder.

He had seen his father often enough wearing the same traditional garments, but quite suddenly he revolted.

"Take them away!" he said harshly. "I will wear the clothes of the gentleman which I am and which I hope to remain!"

When he went down to breakfast he thought that the kilted servants attending him glanced at him with a question in their eyes.

It made him even more determined than ever that he would not pander to the ridiculous nonsense of ancient customs which were "as dead as a door-nail."

Deliberately, so as to avoid mention of the ordeal that lay ahead of him, he said in a conversational tone to Lord Hinchley:

"What do you intend to do with yourself today, William?"

"Something that will make you extremely envious," Lord Hinchley replied. "I am going fishing."

The Duke did not reply and he went on:

"Dunblane tells me there are plenty of salmon in your river, and tomorrow, if you can spare the time, Taran, I should like to have a shot at your grouse."

The fact that his friend intended to do some things he would have liked to do himself did not improve the Duke's temper.

He merely concerned himself with breakfast, which he found, despite a desire to find fault, extremely appetising.

As he was finishing the excellent dish of sea-trout, his nephew Jamie came into the room.

He had had only a brief glance at the boy the evening before, when he arrived, and now he appraised him more critically, noticing that he had red hair and blue eyes.

He found that surprising until he remembered that it was characteristic of the Campbells—the Race of Diamid—and that Jamie's grandmother on his father's side had belonged to that Clan.

As he had obviously been instructed to do, Jamie bowed first to him, then to Lord Hinchley.

"Good-morning, Jamie!" the Duke said perfunctorily.

"It is not a good morning!" Jamie replied hotly. "Jeannie says I should be coming with you today to fight the Kilcraigs, but Mr. Dunblane will not let me."

"I am not going to fight the Kilcraigs," the Duke replied, "so Jeannie, whoever she may be, has been misinformed."

"They are our enemies and we hate them!" Jamie insisted. "You must battle with them as Chief of the McNarns, and I should be with you."

The Duke sighed impatiently.

It seemed that even the child was inoculated with these barbaric customs, for he was well aware that if a Chieftain went into battle his kinsmen accompanied him, besides all the other henchmen whom Dunblane had mentioned last night.

"Now let me make this quite clear," he said firmly. "I am not fighting the Kilcraigs, nor do I intend to do so. Those feuds and hatreds are out-of-date. They are our neighbours and we must learn to live in peace with them."

"In peace with the Kilcraigs?" Jamie exclaimed. "And also the MacAuads?"

"With both!" the Duke said firmly, and concentrated on his breakfast.

He knew that his small nephew was staring at him in surprise and also with what he thought was an expression perilously near contempt.

It was an impertinence, he told himself, that should be severely corrected, but not this morning, not when he had so many other troubles on his hands.

Jamie had, however, started off a train of thought which returned to his mind when he was wending his way up the moors.

Behind the Duke came, as Mr. Dunblane had predicted, a procession of mounted Clansmen, although the Duke knew that in the past they would have walked, with the Piper playing a battle-tune to stir their senses and accelerate their progress.

As it was over a two-hour ride to Kilcraig Castle the Duke was grateful that at least he was permitted to travel there on horse-back, and he guessed that his entourage had been reduced in size to fit the availability of horses to mount them.

Nevertheless, he told himself sourly, there were quite enough, and by the expression on his henchmen's faces they were all as ready as Jamie had been for a fight with their traditional enemy.

The Duke, however, had no intention of doing anything but rescue Torquil, and he hoped to create a new spirit between the Clans which would prevent this sort of thing from happening in the future.

With the MacAuads it was a different cup of tea altogether.

The lands of the McNarns stretched eastwards for many miles and the Clans between them and the sea were either too small to be of any importance or were united by marriage with what amounted to blood ties.

But all through the centuries the MacAuads, a wild, uncouth, and savage Clan, had been an hereditary enemy whom every other Clan hated and feared.

They shared the western border of the McNarn lands with the Kilcraigs, and while the latter were in some way almost a respected enemy, the MacAuads' deeds had put them beyond the pále of any emotion save that of utter loathing.

"Touch a snake and ye'll find a MacAuad!" was a current phrase amongst the Clansmen; another said even more forcefully: "If ye go down to Hell, ye'll find the Devil is MacAuad."

Not having heard of the MacAuads since he was a

boy, the Duke wondered if they were still so ferocious.

He imagined that if there was any cattle-stealing in this part of the world it would be done by the MacAuads, not as a boyish prank but deliberately to enrich themselves at another Clan's expense.

It was a clear day with just a touch of wind, the heather smelt fragrant, and the purple of it was more vivid than the Duke remembered.

There was enough water still left in the burns to make him feel sure that Lord Hinchley would catch several salmon.

It was unfortunate that he could not join his friend but instead was forced to expend his time and energy in visiting a man he had never seen, and in the uncomfortable position of a supplicant.

Then the Duke told himself that The Kilcraig would surely listen to reason.

He supposed that if he paid the full price for the cattle which Torquil had stolen, and perhaps made it more generous than the animals were worth, the whole confrontation would die down.

"Why Dunblane could not have settled the matter for me God only knows!" the Duke muttered beneath his breath.

Then he knew that that was impossible because only a Chief speaking to a Chief could negotiate problems which concerned a Clan, and Dunblane would have no authority despite his long connection with the McNarns.

The Duke's thoughts were back to his position as a Chieftain.

It had been impossible not to notice the solicitousness, which was almost an act of reverence, with which he had been helped onto the saddle of his horse and the way in which the henchmen saluted him.

The women who had been waiting at the gates to

the Castle to see him leave had curtseyed while the Clansmen amongst them had lifted their bonnets and waved them at his approach.

The Duke now remembered when he was a small boy, about the same age as Jamie, saying to his father:

"Why do they love you, Papa?"

His father's answer had been simple:

"I am their Chief."

"What does Chief mean?" the little boy had insisted.

His father, speaking solemnly, almost as if he was thinking aloud, had replied:

"The Highlanders esteem it a most sublime degree of virtue to love their Chief and ply him with a blood obedience, although it be opposition to the Government and the law of the Kingdom, or even the law of God. He is their idol and they know no King but him."

The Duke repeated the words now to himself and he wondered if it was possible to find anywhere else in the world this unquestioning subservience that was not only for the Chief himself but for what he stood for in his followers' imagination.

God knows his father had not deserved such devotion, and yet he had received it just because he was invested with the aura of authority which had been handed down through the centuries.

It was somehow embarrassing, as if one looked into another man's heart and soul.

'The sooner I get back to sanity,' the Duke thought savagely, 'the better!'

He had decided before he left London that he would return South with the King on the *Royal George*.

He knew that His Majesty would be only too pleased to have him and he was quite sure that it would be an amusing voyage. They would all be able to laugh over the incidents that invariably occurred on such occasions.

The King, the Duke knew, was taking his visit very seriously.

Ever since he had decided to go to Scotland he had talked about it with an enthusiasm which surprised those in attendance, who were quite sure that he would be disappointed at what he found in the most northern part of his Kingdom.

But when George IV made up his mind to do something there were few people brave enough to dissuade him and the arrangements had gone ahead.

The Duke supposed that by this time Edinburgh was in a fervour of excitement and anticipation and he certainly had no wish to be there.

He was, however, hot and thirsty by the time they had ridden for over two hours and had the first sight of Kilcraig Castle.

The Duke had never seen it before and he realised that it was a very different building from his own.

From its vantage point on the side of the hill it would have been impossible for an enemy to approach through the valley without being seen and there was something weird and eerie about its high walls with few windows.

Vaguely at the back of his mind the Duke remembered when he was young hearing that the Kilcraigs had ghosts and evil spirits besides ancestors who were cruel monsters, one of them having kidnapped children to use as sacrifices in his sorceries.

The Duke had not believed such stories even when he was a boy, and yet now, looking at the Castle in the distance, he could understand how they had arisen.

There was something about it which stirred the imagination and would, he was quite certain, arouse to wild flights of fancy the superstitions of a primitive people who had been brought up to believe in such things.

The Duke had long ago laughed to scorn the Celtic mythology of giants, witches, unconquerable swordsmen, loch-monsters, precognitions, stones which spoke with the voices of men, and singing trees.

In the South, while few people he knew were concerned with anything but their own amusements, even religion was spoken of with a faint air of mockery.

While the King was obliged to attend Divine Service on Sundays, the Duke and his contemporaries spent their Sundays like any other day, in sport and gaming.

They were within a mile of the Castle when Mr. Dunblane moved his horse beside the Duke's.

"From here, Your Grace," he said in a low voice, "we will all leave our horses, with the exception of yourself."

"Why?" the Duke enquired.

"The Kilcraig, as was your father, is a stickler for custom."

The Duke was about to reply that The Kilcraig could go to Hell, then he told himself that the purpose of the meeting was to be conciliatory, and to anger the old man before it had even started would be foolish.

"Arrange things as you wish, Dunblane," he said curtly and rode on.

He was, however, well aware that the horses were being left in the charge of henchmen and a procession had formed behind him on foot.

First came Dunblane as his immediate body-guard and with him should have been his kinsmen, if Torquil had not been a prisoner of the Kilcraigs and Jamie too young.

Then came the Bard, an old man whom the Duke remembered since his father's time.

Barding was hereditary and carried with it a grant of land. The Highlands had no written history and a man's reputation and the memory of it could mount or fall on the tongue of the Bard.

The Duke wondered wryly what would be said of him when he was dead, and thought it unlikely that his behaviour would inspire an epic poem.

Behind the Bard came the Piper, who now was playing the marching-tune of the McNarns—a tune which led them into battle and accompanied them on their last journey to the cemetery of their forefathers.

Behind the Piper should have been the *Bladier*, the Chief spokesman, a golden-voiced man of debate and argument who knew every precedent in every quarrel.

If he was there he was unnecessary, for the Duke had every intention of speaking for himself and certainly allowing no-one else to interview on his behalf.

Behind these there should have been a gillie to carry his broadsword and buckler and several others who in the past would have been swordsmen, axe-men, bowmen, or musket-men.

It was compulsory for a Clan which was visited by the Chief of another to bed and feed these wild, often savage men without protest.

Except in the case of a Clan like the MacAuads, once having accepted a Clan's hospitality and eaten their salt, there would be no more fighting until they had left the land.

As they drew nearer to Kilcraig Castle the Duke saw the Clansmen waiting for him.

He was surprised to see so many of them wearing the tartan. He had been told in the South that after the ban on it had been lifted in 1799, many of the Scots, after years of persecution by the English, had been too lethargic to reintroduce their own tartan.

Instead they had kept to the anonymous, dark-dyed garments they had worn during the persecution.

The Duke now realised he had made a mistake in not listening to Mr. Dunblane and coming attired in the regalia of a Chieftain.

Then he thought angrily that it did not matter in the least what The Kilcraig or anyone else thought.

They would accept him as he was or be damned to them!

He was received with courtesy but otherwise in silence, and when he dismounted at the door of the Castle he was led by a man resplendent in kilt, badger sporran, and silver-buttoned jacket up a narrow uncarpeted stone staircase to the first floor.

The Duke knew he was being taken to the Chief's Room.

His own Chief's Room, having been redecorated and improved by William Adam, was one of the most impressive and magnificent rooms in the whole building.

He saw at a glance as he entered the Chief's Room of the Kilcraigs that it could be very little changed since the Clansmen had first plotted how to harass and kill their enemies, and bowmen had been on the alert on the Castle turrets to watch for them.

The floor was covered only with fur rugs, and the furniture, of heavy, unpolished oak, would doubtless, if it could talk, have told strange tales.

The windows were narrow so that the sunlight seemed to be excluded, and the great claymores hanging on the walls and the flags and banners captured in battle gave the place a sinister air.

It was easy to believe many of the unpleasant and frightening legends which had grown and multiplied about the Castle down the centuries.

At the far end of the room, in front of a high-backed chair which was almost like a throne, stood The Kilcraig.

The Duke saw that banked on either side of him were his kinsmen, all wearing the Kilcraig tartan.

Again the Duke wished he could rival their splendour and again admitted to himself that he had made a mistake.

Because he resented the show that had been put on to impress if not to intimidate him, he walked languidly down the long room, looking round him with a supercilious air.

He was followed only by Robert Dunblane, the rest of those who accompanied him having been left outside the front door.

He reached The Kilcraig and was annoyed to find that his host stood on a dais which made him half a foot taller than he was in reality.

The Duke was, however, determined to take the initiative and before The Kilcraig could speak he held out his hand.

"We have never had the chance of meeting before, Kilcraig," he said. "May I say that I am delighted to make your acquaintance?"

It was almost with an air of reluctance that The Kilcraig took the Duke's proffered hand.

He was a man of seventy or over, with dead white hair and a beard. He carried his shoulders like a soldier and exuded pride in every inch of his bearing.

"Nay, we've not met before, My Lord Duke," he said, speaking with a broad Scottish accent. "But I welcome you to my Castle."

He released the Duke's hand and introduced him to his sons, his nephews, and then his grandsons.

The Duke knew instinctively that they had no wish to shake his hand, but regarded him warily. He thought too that they were somewhat bewildered by his appearance, looking at him as if he were a strange animal of which they had heard but never seen.

The Kilcraig indicated a chair on the right of his

own, and as the Duke sat down servants brought whisky and set on the table a haggis, bannocks, girdle scones, and other Scottish dishes.

This, the Duke knew, was not luncheon but merely the sort of food that would be offered to a traveller to abate the exhaustion of a long journey.

He drank a little of the whisky and waved away the food. Then, determined once again to take the initiative, he said:

"I think, Kilcraig, we could serve our interests better if we spoke alone on the matter which concerns my visit."

The Chief's heavy white eye-brows shot up.

"Alone?" he queried.

"Why not?" the Duke enquired. "I have the unfair disadvantage of having no kinsmen, while there are so many reinforcements on your side of the table that the odds are heavily against me."

He spoke lightly, with a note of amusement in his voice, and he knew that he surprised The Kilcraig.

"Alone!" the old man repeated under his breath.

"I think between us we can see that justice is done," the Duke said.

The Kilcraig snapped his fingers and without comment his kinsmen filed slowly down the long room and out through the door.

The Duke leant back at his ease.

"That is better!" he said. "And now we can talk as man to man. Shall I start by apologising for the mischievous and very tiresome behaviour of my nephew who, I understand, is somewhat wild and out-of-hand?"

The Kilcraig did not speak but stared at the Duke in a penetrating manner as if he would look beneath the surface of his casual air.

The Duke again sipped his whisky. It was unpleasant, but he was thirsty.

"Torquil McNarn was captured by my men in the act of stealing a valuable animal," The Kilcraig said at length.

"So I have been told," the Duke answered. "It was extremely reprehensible, but no more than a boyish prank."

"It has happened before. Several of the crofters on the borders of my land have complained in the past few months."

"Of losing cattle?"

"In one instance several sheep."

"They must of course be recompensed," the Duke said. "But I am sure you will agree with me that adolescent boys get up to mischief when they have nothing to do, and that is something I intend to remedy in the future."

"What sort of recompense did you have in mind?" The Kilcraig asked.

The Duke made a gesture with his hand.

"Anything you consider adequate for those who have lost their animals."

"My sons insist that Torquil McNarn be sent to Edinburgh and punished by the Courts."

"Surely that is making rather heavy weather over what is nothing very serious?" the Duke questioned. "The days of feuding and the demand for vengeance by our Clans are over."

"Do you think that is possible?" The Kilcraig asked.

"Of course!" the Duke replied. "The world has become more enlightened. The feuds of the past are as out-of-date as the Dodo!"

"It is a pity you cannot say that to the MacAuads!"

The Duke wondered why the MacAuads had been introduced into the conversation.

"I remember that years ago they were always up to some devilment," he said reflectively. "They have not changed in any way?"

"If anything they are worse!" The Kilcraig answered. "I am prepared to admit there was no question of the McNarns as a Clan conniving with your nephew, but where the MacAuads are concerned they attack your Clan and mine, not in isolated instances, but continuously, viciously, and with premeditated violence!"

"I can hardly believe that!" the Duke exclaimed.

"It is true," The Kilcraig said, "and that is why, Duke, I have a proposition to put to you."

"A proposition?" the Duke questioned.

"I have been thinking over this for some time," The Kilcraig said slowly, "and the behaviour of Torquil McNarn has only accelerated a decision I have come to reluctantly but of necessity."

"And what is that?" the Duke enquired.

"It is that if we are to withstand the assaults of the MacAuads, then your Clan and mine should become affiliated by the oath of friendship."

The Duke looked at the old man in sheer astonishment.

In his wildest imagination he had never expected that such a proposition would have come from The Kilcraig.

All his boyhood he had been brought up to consider him a natural enemy, not in the same category as the MacAuads, but nevertheless an enemy.

He had hoped to create a better relationship between the Clans but nothing as sweeping as this.

There was silence until he managed to say:

"Do you really believe such a solution is possible?"

"I think it is not only possible but imperative!" The Kilcraig answered. "We cannot go on as we are. Your nephew has taken some cattle from us, but that is nothing to what is happening on our borders which march with the MacAuads."

His voice deepened with anger as he went on:

"Some of our more prosperous farmers have even paid blackmail, but the MacAuads in their treachery not only took the mail but waited for a moonlit night and took the animals as well!"

He struck the table and continued:

"Only by guarding every mile of our land can I protect my own people, but the burden is growing too heavy. The marauding thieves get through, however much we try to stop them."

"And you think the McNarns would help you?" the Duke asked.

"Look at the map," The Kilcraig answered. "If we combine we will be twice the size, it not more, of the MacAuads."

"I suppose that is true," the Duke murmured.

"They are not only thieves and bullies, treacherous and without honour, they are also leaderless," The Kilcraig answered. "Their Chief prefers the soft living of the South, like many others who have deserted those who trust them."

The old man paused, then said:

"A Clan without a Chief is like a ship without a rudder."

The Duke was silent. After a moment The Kilcraig asked:

"Will you listen to my proposition, My Lord Duke?"

"I am very willing to do so," the Duke answered.

"It is this," The Kilcraig said. "I will release Torquil McNarn and the three youths with him. I will give you my sacred oath on the dirk that the Kilcraigs will live in peace with the McNarns, and you will give me yours. To make sure that all those who follow us know that the hand of friendship wipes out the blood that has been shed between us, you will marry my daughter!"

For a moment the Duke felt he could not have heard The Kilcraig aright.

It was with an effort that he prevented his mouth from dropping open in sheer surprise.

Then in a voice which sounded strange even to himself he asked:

"Did you say that I should—marry your daughter?"

"She is of marriageable age, but I have not yet found a husband for her," The Kilcraig said. "As the Duchess of Strathnarn she will be respected by both our own people and yours. There will be no problems between us in the future and we can concentrate on repressing the MacAuads."

It all sounded extremely reasonable, the Duke thought, as set forth in the deep, slow voice of The Kilcraig.

Then he told himself he had no intention of marrying anyone, least of all a raw, uncivilised Scottish girl, who as far as he was concerned was as remote from his chosen way of life as an Aborigine from Australia.

Aloud he said:

"I certainly agree to your idea of uniting our Clans to our mutual benefit, but I am sure you will understand that I have no intention of marrying anyone, preferring for the time being at any rate to remain a bachelor."

The Kilcraig pushed back his chair.

"In which case, Your Grace, there is no point in continuing this conversation. Torquil McNarn will go to trial and doubtless the Judges in Edinburgh will not be overly hard on him."

The Duke did not rise. He merely sat still, his eyes on the old Chief, trying to think of a way out of this impasse.

"Surely," he said in a conciliatory tone, "the fact that I am prepared to agree to the oath of friendship is a step forward that does not need my private involvement to the extent of marriage."

The Kilcraig did not move. He merely said:

"First, I doubt if your Clan or mine will accept that things are greatly changed without a physical sign that we are affiliated closer than can be shown by words."

The Duke had to acknowledge that this was very likely the truth. What was more, as the majority of the Highlanders could not read, there would be some difficulty in making them understand exactly what was involved unless they had a wedding, or some equally sensational ceremony in which to take part.

"Secondly," The Kilcraig went on, "what is to stop you, once Torquil McNarn has been handed over to you, from repudiating our arrangement?"

"Would you doubt my word of honour?" the Duke asked sharply.

The Kilcraig smiled cynically—it was little more than raising the corners of his thin lips.

"It has happened in the past. You will remember that in 1423 your ancestor made a bargain with mine not to invade the northern approaches to our land."

This was a piece of history that the Duke had forgotten, if he had ever heard of it.

"The Kilcraigs were relaxed and at their ease," the old Chief went on, "and the McNarns, creeping through the heather, took them by surprise. They killed fifty of our Clansmen, raped their women, and carried off their cattle."

There was a note in the Chief's voice which told the Duke that the act of treachery was as vivid and real to him as if it had happened yesterday.

"I have therefore made up my mind," The Kilcraig continued, "that only by a marriage between you and my daughter will peace come to our troubled people."

"Are you seriously telling me," the Duke asked,

"that if I do not agree fully to what you suggest you will send my nephew to Edinburgh?"

"My men are waiting to escort him there," The Kilcraig said, "and my eldest son will lay his crime before the Justices."

The Duke was still.

He knew that if he abandoned Torquil and those with him to their fate he would not only find it impossible to face his Clansmen but his own name would be dragged through the dust.

He imagined how quickly the Press in Edinburgh would become aware of the fact that the Duke of Strathnarn's nephew and heir was in the dock as a common thief.

The publicity would doubtless coincide with the visit of the King, and the Duke thought he would be a laughing-stock not only to all the other Scottish noblemen but to his English friends who were to accompany His Majesty to Edinburgh.

He felt like a cornered rat and it seemed to him there was no possible escape.

To play for time he asked rather feebly:

"Is your daughter in agreement with this proposition?"

"My daughter does as she is told, as do all my family," The Kilcraig answered. "She will serve you with the same obedience and loyalty she has given to me."

The Duke thought that if he was in his right senses he would rise to his feet and tell The Kilcraig that this was blackmail of the worst type and he had no intention of submitting to it.

Then he knew that the old man was as obstinate and determined as his father would have been and that nothing would budge him once he had made up his mind.

It was part of the spirit of the Scots, who would die

rather than surrender, who would fight to their last breath rather than admit defeat.

For a moment the Duke wondered if he was dreaming and would wake to find himself in his house in London with no more important decision to make than in which style he should tie his cravat.

He wanted to play for time, to discuss his predicament with someone cleverer than himself.

Then he knew without asking that The Kilcraig would not wait. He had already said that the Clansmen were ready to escort Torquil to Edinburgh, and the Duke was sure he had not lied.

He looked at the rugged countenance of the Chief and saw a granite-like hardness that recalled the past.

It was how his father had looked when he was determined to beat him into submission, when he gave orders that he was forced to obey because he had not the strength to fight him.

Almost as if it came to him from a far distance he heard his own voice saying:

"If I agree to your suggestion, Kilcraig, will you allow me to take back with me my nephew and those whom you hold?"

The Kilcraig made no movement; only his voice, quiet yet authoritative, replied:

"Torquil McNarn will come to your wedding, which I suggest should be held at the same time as you receive the homage not only of your own Clan but also of mine."

"But that, I believe, is scheduled to take place in the next day or so," the Duke protested.

He remembered that Mr. Dunblane had intimated that the McNarns were gathering from all parts of his land and he had known without being told what this would entail.

"Exactly!" The Kilcraig said. "And because yours is the older Clan, Clola will be married at your Castle, and you will present her to both our people at the same time."

It was a clever idea, the Duke thought, and he knew The Kilcraig must have been cogitating over it and thinking out every detail for a long time.

The ghastly thing was, he could think of no possible way to prevent it from taking place.

There must be something he could say, some loophole, some escape, he told himself, and felt his mind turning over and over in an effort to free himself from a noose which seemed to be tightening round his throat.

"I suppose. . . " he began.

The Kilcraig moved impatiently.

"Will you eat with us, Duke?" he asked. "Or would you be on your way home?"

It was an ultimatum and the Duke had the feeling that whichever way he decided there would be no appeal, no second chance, no possible way in which he could extricate himself.

He longed as he had never longed in his life before to hurl defiance at The Kilcraig and tell him to do his worst.

Then he knew it was impossible—impossible to betray his own blood, impossible to wash his hands of the inevitable consequences.

Slowly and with dignity he rose to his feet.

"I am extremely hungry, Kilcraig," he replied.

* * *

Afterwards as they rode home the Duke could remember only the expression of sheer astonishment on Robert Dunblane's face when after their meal was finished The Kilcraig announced to his kinsmen who had sat at the table with them the decision which had been reached.

If Mr. Dunblane was surprised, so were they.

"Join with the McNarns?" one of The Kilcraig's older sons enquired.

Although he spoke quietly it might have been a yell of savage protest.

"This is our only chance to control the MacAuads," The Kilcraig replied.

The men did not mention their sister Clola, but the Duke knew by their uneasy glances that they were thinking of her.

Finally The Kilcraig toasted the Duke and the Duke was forced to toast him in return.

"May our hearts be as closely united as our hands and our tongues," The Kilcraig said finally in Gaelic.

With an effort the Duke managed to answer in the same language:

"May your wish come true."

He was bemused, bewildered, and only as he rode away from Kilcraig Castle, followed by his procession with the bag-pipes swirling out, did he remember that he had not in fact seen his future bride.

For a moment he tightened the reins and brought his horse to a standstill.

Surely it was an omission that was not only fantastic from his own point of view but also an insult to the woman he was to marry.

Then he told himself that if The Kilcraig had meant them to meet, he would have suggested it.

The old Chief had been, the Duke thought furiously, in complete command of the whole situation from the very beginning.

He had had everything planned in his mind, he had been determined to have his own way, and he had succeeded without any opposition.

"I am weak, feeble, puerile!" the Duke flayed himself.

But he still found it was impossible to think of any means by which he could have refused The Kilcraig without sacrificing not only Torquil but his own pride and honour.

Once or twice already there had been various scurrilous reports written about him in the newspapers in London, and a cartoon had depicted one of his amatory adventures in a manner which had made him grind his teeth.

It had been nothing half as bad as what was said about the King, who paid the cartoonists "hush-money."

At the same time, something savage and unrestrained in the Duke had made him feel as if he was prepared to run his sword through the body of the artist who had lampooned him or blow his brains out with a bullet from his duelling-pistol.

He had in fact taken part in quite a number of duels, and, although he had never killed a man, he had come perilously near to it in one instance.

He thought now as he rode across the heather that it would give him great pleasure to be present at The Kilcraig's funeral, however much the old man might enjoy himself at his wedding.

He wanted to swear aloud to relieve his furious conviction that he had been out-manoeuvred by a very clever antagonist.

Although he might be The Kilcraig's superior as a Chieftain, he was certainly his inferior when it came to brain-power.

Could it be possible that this uncivilised savage, Chief of a Clan of which South of the border nobody had ever heard, was shrewd enough to humiliate the dashing, much-admired sportsman who was a friend of the King?

He knew that he held a position amongst the other Bucks and Dandies of St. James's that was almost unique.

He was aware that he was sought out by Statesmen

and older men because of the wit and intelligence of his conversation, and certainly as far as women were concerned for his other attractions.

Yet within twenty-four hours of landing in Scotland he had been out-witted, out-manoeuvred, and treated as a pawn in the hand of a man who he was quite certain had never travelled South of Edinburgh.

It was impossible for the Duke to speak to Mr. Dunblane of what he was suffering.

When he arrived back at the Castle to find Lord Hinchley delighted with himself for having caught three salmon, he told him briefly what had occurred.

"You have to marry this woman?" Lord Hinchley ejaculated. "I do not believe you!"

"It is true!"

"Good God! I would not have believed that such a thing was possible if you had not told me so with your own lips."

"You must see that I have no alternative!"

"It is inhuman! Barbaric! Just what I should have expected of these savages!"

"What could I do?" the Duke asked.

"I do realise that it was impossible for you to abandon the boy, but to have to marry a woman you have never seen. . . !"

"It would make it no better if I had," the Duke said gloomily.

He sounded so depressed that Lord Hinchley rose from where he was sitting to pour out a glass of brandy and hand it to the Duke.

"There is only one consolation," he said slowly as he did so.

"What is that?" the Duke asked, with not a flicker of hope in his voice.

"You will have to marry her—I see that," Lord Hinchley replied. "Then get her with child and leave her. Come South and forget the whole incident."

He paused before he added in a more cheerful voice:

"After all, the fact that you are married should certainly not restrict your activities in London. The last dozen women with whom you amused yourself all had husbands."

"I suppose that is true," the Duke admitted.

"Then why worry?" Lord Hinchley asked. "Married or unmarried, they will still find you the best-looking and most amusing man in London, and Scotland will be very far away."

"As you say, William, Scotland will be very far away," the Duke repeated.

He raised his glass.

"I shall be able to drink not to absent friends but to my absent wife—and may she never come South!"

Chapter Three

Clola Kilcraig stared at herself in the mirror and thought it was impossible that this should be her wedding-day.

Ever since her father had told her she was to marry the Duke of Strathnarn she had felt that she was living in a dream and would wake to find that it was all a figment of her imagination, which her family had often threatened would get her into trouble.

She had been a dreamer all her life, and to her the superstitions and legends not only of the Kilcraigs but also of the other Clans were part of the mountains, the glens, the burns, and the moors that she loved.

She had listened when she was small to the stories her Nurse had told her of snow-maidens, elves, and ghosts, and thought she heard and saw them.

When she grew older she had sat at the feet of the Bard while he recited long poems which bored her brothers but which she found entrancing and stimulating to her thoughts and feelings.

There were books at the Castle that had accumulated over the years, but no-one read them or was even aware of their existence, except for Clola.

Only when she went to Edinburgh to stay with her grandmother had she found in literature all that she vaguely sensed within herself but had not been able to put into words.

Her visits to Edinburgh had, she realised, altered her whole life in a way she could never explain to her brothers without hurting their pride and their belief that the whole world began and ended on their own lands.

They had been to school and Edinburgh University but they had hated every moment of it and had lived only to return to their farming and to obeying their father implicitly because he had not only bred them but was also their Chieftain.

Clola had visited Edinburgh first with her mother when she was twelve.

It had been difficult for Lady Janet Kilcraig to see much of her family, whose lands lay South of Edinburgh and were therefore inaccessible at many times of the year, owing to the roughness of the roads.

But the Countess of Borrabul had written, saying that she was ill, and even The Kilcraig could not forbid his wife to visit her mother, who might be near to death.

Lady Janet had therefore taken her youngest daughter with her and set off on the long and arduous drive to Edinburgh, the roads being at times a morass of mud and at other times under water from swollen burns and flooded lochs.

But they had reached the city safely, and Clola would never forget how impressed she had been with the thousand-year-old Castle standing on a great rock, the wide, busy streets, the Palace with its memories of Mary, Queen of Scots, and the elegance of the people she met.

The Countess, who seemed in surprisingly good health considering that she had written so dramatically to demand her daughter's presence, had exclaimed in horror when she saw her clothes and the rough garments worn by Clola.

"They are suitable enough, Mama, for the life we lead," Lady Janet Kilcraig had protested.

But the Countess had ordered dressmakers, furriers, milliners, and shoe- and glove-makers to call, and had made long lists of what they would require.

Clola and her mother had been fitted out in beautiful, expensive gowns, which they knew would be quite useless when they returned home.

In Edinburgh for the first time Clola had heard music that was not played on the bag-pipes, and she listened to intelligent people who talked about things other than feuds, vengeance, and the price of cattle.

She had cried when she was obliged to return home, and her grandmother when kissing her good-bye had said over her head:

"This child must be properly educated. She will be a beauty when she grows up, but who is going to see her but grouse and stags if you keep her shut up in that gloomy, ghost-ridden Castle of yours?"

Her mother had laughed, but when three years later she died, the Countess of Borrabul, by using the excuse that she might not live long, had persuaded The Kilcraig to send Clola to Edinburgh.

For nearly three years Clola had lived a life that was so completely different from everything she had known previously that it had a special magic of its own.

Not the magic of the mountains and the moors, but a magic nevertheless, in that she could feel her mind expanding and broadening as she learnt the subjects which before had been incomprehensible.

Most important of all, she could listen to the Concerts that were given at the Theatre in Edinburgh and even occasionally hear an Opera.

She was not, however, allowed to go to school; for that, the Countess had told her, was not correct for daughters of the nobility, wherever their brothers might be sent.

But she had had teachers for every subject and she thought there was so much history round her that it was almost unnecessary to open the books on it.

When she was eighteen and had been launched into Society the previous winter, the tragedy her grandmother had so often used as a pretext to get her own way happened, and the Countess died, leaving Clola to return home.

She had not forgotten what the Castle meant in her life. She had not ceased to love her brothers and even her father, although she was afraid of him. But she knew, when she was honest with herself, that life at home was going to be restrictive.

She would not feel as she had felt in Edinburgh that her mind, like her imagination, had wings which would carry her up into the sky.

She found, however, that her years in the city had given her a deeper appreciation of the beauty of the mountains and wild moors that had been so much a part of her childhood.

Sitting in the heather, she could look out over the glen beneath her and hear music on the breeze and feel that it carried a special message to her heart, as even the great orchestras she had listened to in Edinburgh had been unable to do.

Apart from her imagination and a certain perception which her old Nurse had told her made her "fey," Clola had a practical side.

On arrival at the Castle she put away her silken gowns and allowed her sisters-in-law and the servants to weave for her home-spun garments in which she could climb the hills or ford a burn without their coming to any harm.

She had also been intelligent enough to assimilate herself quickly into the family circle, keeping her newfound knowledge to herself and listening to her brothers with an attention which both pleased and flattered them.

She felt at times that her father sensed she was not as complaisant as he required, and although she had never defied him she knew perceptively that he expected her sometime to do so.

In fact, the first time during the three months since her return home that she had been involved in an argument with him was after the Duke had left.

Like everyone else in the Castle, Clola had been excited at the thought of his visit. She had been told when Torquil McNarn was captured what a score it was over their enemies the McNarns.

Having heard noises the previous night and wondered what was occurring, she was actually surprised and horrified when she learnt the following morning at breakfast what had occurred.

It was her elder brother Andrew who told her that they had waited in the darkness on the border of their land to capture Torquil McNarn and three other lads in the very act of thieving.

"Thieving?" Clola had questioned.

"Not for the first time," Andrew replied. "But now he'll pay the penalty. I have always hoped to catch a man in the act, but I did not expect such a prize prisoner as the Duke's nephew!"

"Surely the McNarns will be very angry?" Clola said.

"Undoubtedly," Andrew replied. "And now we will wait to see what they do about it."

Clola had clasped her hands together in horror.

She hated the thought of fighting, violence, and

bloodshed. There had been far too much of it in their history.

But she knew that if she objected, her brothers would merely despise her for her weakness and, what was more, would ignore any protest she might make.

To them, a woman's place was in the home, looking after her babies and superintending the kitchen and the Still-Room. If she had time on her hands she would weave and spin as the Scottish womenfolk had done since the beginning of time.

But at least Torquil's capture had given them something different to talk about and had brought new visitors to the Castle.

First had come Mr. Dunblane and the fathers of the three boys who had been captured at the same time as Torquil McNarn.

Clola had not been allowed to be present at their meeting with her father, but she had watched them arrive and had peeped at them as they ascended the stairs to the Chief's Room.

She had thought Mr. Dunblane looked charming and very like some of the interesting, intelligent men she had met in Edinburgh.

The Clansmen with him had stared at The Kilcraig, who had glared back, and Clola was sure it was only by the greatest exertion of self-control that they were not at one another's throats.

She had almost forgotten in Edinburgh how violent the feuds between the neighbouring Clans could be and how the hatred that had been engendered could easily make a man into a murderer.

When Mr. Dunblane had ridden away she had learnt that her father had refused to negotiate with anyone but the Chieftain of the McNarns, the Duke of Strathnarn.

She had heard him spoken of when she was in Edinburgh.

She knew that he had run away from home when he was sixteen because he could not tolerate his father's discipline and that he now lived in the South.

Her father had the utmost contempt for the Duke's maternal grandfather, who, although he was a Scot, was a Lowlander and had not taken part in the Jacobite Rebellion. Instead, he had accepted the favours of the English and was welcomed at the Court of St. James.

"A renegade! A traitor! A man who has betrayed his own people!" were just some of the insults hurled by The Kilcraig at him and all Scots like him.

But in Edinburgh Clola had begun to understand why so many Chieftains found the life of the Highlands too hard and too restrictive for them.

In the previous centuries the Chiefs had been men of contradictions, civilised savages whose interests and experiences were often wider than most Englishmen's.

Many of them could speak Gaelic, English, and French, as well as Greek and Latin, and they had sent their sons to be educated at Universities in Glasgow, Edinburgh, Paris, and Rome.

They had come back wearing lace at their throats, with a liking for French claret, and able to dance the Highland reels as well as the minuets of the South.

To the French and indeed to the English, the Chieftains had been attractive and rather picturesque foreigners.

When they were with their Clans they were Kings, but of very small Kingdoms and with few amusements other than shooting and fishing, Bardic poems and wild pipe-music.

For the earlier Chieftains, in the sixteenth century, there had been continuous Clan battles and cattle-raids to occupy them.

There had also been hunting on the high mountains where in those days stags, wolves, and cats abounded.

Deer-hunts with cross-bows and broadswords were a spectacle which the Bards would re-create in the long, dark winter evenings when there was nothing to do but sit round the great peat fires.

But the Chieftains who had travelled were beginning to find it a bore to return to their own country.

In one way Clola could sympathise with them, but she knew that a Clan without its Chieftain was helpless and, like the MacAuads, deteriorated until the words "savage" and "barbarian" were an apt description.

When she thought of this Clola began to be afraid that the soothsayers' predictions of the curse that would come upon the Highlands and the suffering and misery which would ensue from it would come true.

It would be called, she had been told,*Bliadhna Nan Caorach*—"The Years of the Sheep."

When she was in Edinburgh she had learnt that successful sheep-farming in the far North had resulted first in large-scale emigration to Canada, and how when other Highlanders refused to emigrate they were evicted.

News travelled slowly.

In Edinburgh the public had not been alerted to what was happening in Sutherland until after Clola had come to live with her grandmother.

Then people talked of little else and every day brought further tales of crofts being burnt over defenceless heads, of cruelties which lost nothing in the telling, and the determination of many Highland Chiefs to follow the lead set by the Marquis of Stafford in Sutherland.

Riots followed the evictions in Ross, and the more people talked, the more Clola's heart began to be wrung with the thought of those who had been forgotten and betrayed by their Chieftains.

They lived, she was told, in caves by the seashore

or were forced aboard the ships which carried them, defenceless and half-starved, to the other side of the world.

She began to understand as she never had before what her father meant to the Clansmen who followed him, and she knew that for him to betray his own people in such a manner would be unthinkable.

She was sure that when her father died Andrew would take his place and be the guide and leader of the Kilcraigs in exactly the same way.

But she could not help wondering whether the Marquis of Narn, whom she had heard spoken of in Edinburgh, would return from the South to take the place of his father, the Duke of Strathnarn.

Several of the gentlemen whom her grandmother entertained had met the Marquis in London.

They spoke of his success on the Turf, of his expertise at driving a Phaeton drawn by six horses, and also of his attraction for women.

The latter was of course not spoken of openly in Clola's presence. Their voices would be lowered when they discussed such things with her grandmother, who delighted in learning of the scandals and the *affaires de coeur* which took place at Carlton House.

Yet, invariably when such whispered conversations took place, Clola heard the name Narn repeated and rerepeated.

When Mr. Dunblane had left and The Kilcraig had told his family that he would not negotiate the release of Torquil McNarn except with the Chief of his Clan, Clola had asked:

"Now that the old Duke is dead, the Chief will be the Marquis of Narn?"

"That is right," The Kilcraig agreed.

"But he is in the South. Will he come North?"

She thought there was a faint twinkle in her father's eye as he replied confidently:

"He will come!"

"How can you be sure?" she persisted. "Supposing like other Chieftains he prefers the South?"

"He will come!" The Kilcraig repeated.

"You really think this incident of cattle-stealing will force him to return to his own people?" Andrew questioned.

Clola had been surprised that her brother appreciated the situation, because she thought from all she had heard it was very unlikely that the Marquis had any interested in Scotland or Scottish affairs.

"Blood is thicker than water," The Kilcraig said. "The Chieftain of the McNarns will come home!"

He had been right, and it had been exciting!

Long before the Duke's ship had docked in Perth, the Kilcraigs as well as his own Clan were aware that he was on his way.

Clola was not surprised, as visitors to Scotland were, that somehow without newspapers everyone always knew what was happening in other Clans, even though they hated one another and did not speak.

Her father knew the very hour that the Duke would arrive; and when the day after his arrival a messenger from Narn Castle came with a letter, Clola sensed an atmosphere of triumph in the very air.

With the other women in the Castle she watched the Duke's approach.

The others were scandalised by the fact that he was not wearing the customary kilt.

"A Chieftain dressed like a Sassenach!" they scoffed. "Does he mean to insult us?"

They speculated amongst themselves as to whether The Kilcraig would refuse to see him, but to Clola the Duke seemed very elegant and exactly as she had expected him to look.

She had known he would be handsome and as tall as, if not taller than, her brothers. She had been sure he would also have an air of authority and consequence that they had never achieved.

There had been many handsome Scots in Edinburgh who moved with a pride and assurance which was somehow different from that of those who came from the South. But the Duke surpassed them all.

When Clola watched him walk from the Chief's Room at her father's side she had thought that the McNarns were fortunate in having a Chieftain worthy of their long history and the deeds of valour which had been attributed to their forefathers.

As the Duke rode away she had watched from an upper window until she saw the procession behind him mount their horses. Then with a little sigh she went down the twisting stone stairs to be told that her father wished to speak to her.

Because he had summoned her to the Chief's Room she expected that what he had to say might be of significance, but his actual words had rung in her ears like the firing of a cannon.

"In three days' time you are to marry the Chief of the McNarns," The Kilcraig announced briefly.

For a moment Clola was speechless. Then she asked:

"D-do you . . . mean the . . . Duke of Strathnarn? B-but . . . why?"

Her father then told her the terms he had imposed for the release of Torquil McNarn.

Clola drew in her breath.

"How could you . . . ask such a thing of him?" she enquired. "And how, indeed, can he . . . agree?"

"If he had not agreed, his nephew and your brother Andrew would be setting out for Edinburgh at this moment with those who would give evidence against him."

"But, Father, I cannot . . . marry like that. It is . . .

wrong. It is not a . . . civilised way of doing such a thing."

Her father looked at her from under his eye-brows in the searching manner which had always made her afraid as a child.

"Are you challenging my decision, Clola?" he enquired.

"You know, Father, that I am always prepared to do as you wish," Clola answered. "At the same time, surely this is too precipitate. Could any marriage succeed in such circumstances? I have not even met the Duke."

"There will be plenty of time after you are married to get to know each other," The Kilcraig said, "and it would be difficult to gather the Clansmen together for a second time when they are engaged on the harvest."

Clola knew that this was true. To show their allegiance to their new leader, the McNarns would be coming now from all over their territory.

For many it would be a long and tiring journey, and they would be forced to leave their wives to look after their cattle and to bring in what harvest was ready.

They would certainly resent, if they did not find it impossible, having to leave home a second time for the marriage of their Chieftain in the months before the winter made it difficult for them to travel.

She could appreciate the practicality of what her father had decided. At the same time, her instinct told her that from her personal point of view and from that of the Duke it was intolerable.

"Please . . . Father, I do not . . . wish to be . . . married in such haste," she pleaded.

"You will obey me," The Kilcraig replied, and she knew that nothing she could say, nothing she could do, would have any influence on him.

What was more, as the Duke had agreed to what

her father had asked, she knew that the joining of the Clans was a victory that nothing would make him forgo.

"Unfortunately, there will be no time for a trousseau," Andrew's wife had said almost gleefully. "But you have enough already to last you for a dozen years or more."

She was usually a placid woman and made Andrew a good wife, but it would have been impossible for any woman not to feel envious of the great trunkloads of clothes which Clola had brought home with her from Edinburgh.

Her grandmother's one great extravagance had been clothes: she loved the new fashions, which thrilled her in the same way that her granddaughter was thrilled by music; and a new style of the hair would bring a light to her eyes even when she was ill.

When she was almost on her death-bed she had said to Clola:

"Do not waste the things in my wardrobe. Take them with you when you return home. You can easily refashion the gowns, and the wraps trimmed with fur will keep you warm."

There was a faintly sarcastic note in her voice, as if she remembered the bleakness of the Castle where her granddaughter would live after her death, and because she only wished to please her grandmother Clola had done as she had asked.

She had thought as she travelled northwards that she would give her sister-in-law anything she desired from her plenteous wardrobe.

But on arrival she found that her own gowns were far too small for her, as were those that had belonged to her grandmother, who had grown thin in her old age.

What was more, Clola realised that she would consider it an insult to be offered clothes that had been worn by somebody else.

Her ball-gowns, and the silks, satins, and muslins which she had worn in the afternoons, were therefore left in the trunks, ready now, she thought, to be carried just as they were over the moors to Narn Castle.

Fortunately, and it would have been surprising if she had not, she had a dress that would be very appropriate as a wedding-gown.

Her grandmother had bought it for her with a number of others, a few weeks before her death, because she had learnt of the likelihood of George IV coming to Edinburgh.

The date had not been settled but the rumour had spread like wildfire, and at the first mention of such a tremendously important occasion her grandmother had had the dressmakers come round and had ordered gowns for herself and for Clola.

She was too weak at the time to do anything but superintend the fitting from her bed.

Although her Doctors had shaken their heads and said it was too much excitement, Clola knew it gave her great pleasure, and she stood for hours, fitting the gowns, enduring endless amendments, additions, and alterations.

She could not help feeling when her grandmother died that it was desperately sad that she should not have had the pleasure of being in Edinburgh for all the festivities that were planned to welcome the King.

No-one would have enjoyed them more; no lady, she felt, would have been more outstanding. But by the time the date for the King's arrival was fixed, her grandmother was already buried and Clola was back at home at Kilcraig.

Now she looked at the gown lying on the bed in the small room that she occupied in one of the towers.

Two storeys above her was Torquil McNarn's

prison. He had been confined there in solitude since the night he had been brought to the Castle.

Clola had suggested that she might visit him, but her brother Andrew had been horrified and had said harshly:

"We will not have you talking to a McNarn!"

"He is only a boy," Clola protested, "and it must be very lonely for him up there."

"He will fare far worse in a prison in Edinburgh," Andrew answered savagely, and the others laughed.

Hamish, however, who was Clola's youngest brother, and about the same age as Torquill McNarn, had whispered to her later:

"Don't worry about our prisoner, Clola. He's all right."

"How do you know?" she asked.

"I've seen him!"

"You have done that? I thought Andrew kept the key to his room."

"I know where he hides it," Hamish said with a grin. "So I've talked to Torquil McNarn and I took him one or two things to make him more comfortable."

"That was kind of you."

"He was unlucky," Hamish answered. "I've got away with what he did half a dozen times!"

"You mean you have stolen from the McNarns?" Hamish grinned at her.

"Of course! It's a fine sport as long as one isn't caught."

"Oh, Hamish, how could you do anything so dangerous?" Clola exclaimed. "If Father knew, he would be furious!"

"I bet he does know," Hamish answered. "But he wouldn't stop me getting the better of the McNarns. It's the MacAuads he's afraid of."

"Afraid?" Clola questioned.

Hamish looked over his shoulder as if he was scared that someone might be listening.

"They broke a man's back last week and killed two of our Clansmen last year."

Clola gave a little cry.

"Father told us not to speak of it, but you can understand why he hates them."

"I can indeed. But I am sorry for Torquil McNarn; he must be afraid of what is going to happen to him."

"Yes, he's afraid all right. He doesn't think his uncle will come to his rescue. He says they all know how much he loathes Scotland."

"I have always been told that the Duke's father was cruel to him," Clola said.

"He beat him until he ran away," Hamish agreed. "One thing about Father, he doesn't often beat us."

It was true, Clola thought, that The Kilcraig's authority rested not on his physical strength, but on his personality, which dominated his family and his Clan.

He had only to look at one of his sons or his henchmen in disapproval and they shook in their shoes.

She could understand, if the new Duke had been as proud as her brothers were, how much he would have resented the humiliation of being beaten.

Hamish then told her of Torquil's reaction to the news that the Clans were to be united and she was to marry his uncle.

"He didn't believe me at first," he related. "Then he said scornfully, 'My uncle would never marry a Kilcraig!'

" 'You don't suppose my sister wants to marry a stuck-up polecat of a McNarn?' I answered."

Clola gave a little cry.

"Oh, Hamish, you did not say that! If he repeats it to his uncle it will make things more difficult for me than they are already."

"How do you know they'll be difficult?" Hamish asked. "You've not met him yet."

"How would you like to be told to marry one of the McNarn women whether you liked it or not?"

"I would slit my throat first," Hamish answered.

Clola laughed.

"I promise you that is something which will never happen."

"You never know," her brother said gloomily. "Only father could have thought of anything so fantastic as our being united with the McNarns after all the years we have fought them and all the things we have said about them."

"I expect they feel the same," Clola answered philosophically. "And what we have to do, you included, Hamish, is to see that the bargain works. You know as well as I do that the fights between the two Clans and the stealing of each other's cattle means only misery and worse poverty than there is already."

"Those McNarns won't change any more than a wild-cat can change his stripes," Hamish grumbled.

Clola had laughed and kissed him because he was too young to understand the deeper issues as she was trying to do.

Only now did she realise that in a few moments she would be leaving her family and the Castle in which she had been born, and she felt desperately afraid of what the future held.

She could understand that her father's plan would be for the benefit of both Clans and would certainly safe-guard those who lived on the border where their lands joined.

But what he had forgotten, she thought, was the human element, and she wondered how long it would be before the McNarns could accept the Kilcraigs as brothers-in-arms and vice versa.

Over her relationship with the Duke was a

question-mark which made her tremble to think of it.

With a sigh she put on an attractive summer habit in which she would ride across the moor.

She had some difficulty in making her father realise that it would be impossible for her to ride a horse for two hours in her wedding-gown without arriving hot and dishevelled at the Castle where she was to be married.

He might have planned everything else to his satisfaction, but she was well aware that he had not thought of her as a woman but merely as a weapon in his hands to force the Duke into accepting the terms he had suggested.

Now as a woman she protested volubly.

"I will not, Father, I repeat *not*, whatever you may say, arrive with my gown creased, my slippers dirty, and my hair blown about my face!"

"Women! Women!" The Kilgraig exclaimed in disgust.

But he gave in and finally sent a messenger to Mr. Dunblane to ask where Clola could change and where the Kilcraig Clansmen could assemble.

To gather them together a fiery cross had been sent across-country. This consisted of two burnt or burning sticks to which was tied a strip of linen, traditionally stained with blood.

This item was omitted on this occasion, but the cross was still passed from hand to hand as if by runners in a relay.

Clola knew that one of the last occasions on which the fiery cross had been sent was when Lord Glenorchy rallied his father's people against the Jacobites in 1745.

Then it had travelled thirty-two miles round Loch Tay in three hours.

She was aware that a Clan that had been gathered

by the cross was moved by deep and ancient superstitions.

A stag, fox, hare, or any beast or game that was seen by the runners and not killed promised evil.

If a bare-foot woman crossed the road before the marching men rallied by the fiery cross, she was seized and blood was drawn from her forehead by the point of a knife.

When Clola learnt that her father intended to send the fiery cross, knowing that no Clansman would refuse to obey its message, she had with her own hands overhauled the strip of linen which held the sticks together, changing it to a bow of white satin ribbon in which she fixed two pieces of white heather.

The men might scoff at it but she knew it would interest and excite the women.

It would be a bitter blow that for most of them it would be impossible to leave their children and the harvest to join their husbands as they rallied to their Chieftain.

Mr. Dunblane's reply to what Clola had thought of as a cry for help had been to say that the Manse was at her disposal and the Kilcraig Clansmen could also gather there the night before or as early in the morning as they wished.

Clola was to ride across the moors, while the long journey involving nearly four hours by road was to be undertaken by her sister-in-law and her small children in a carriage.

"You would be more comfortable with us," she suggested, but Clola shook her head.

"It is far quicker on horse-back," she said, "and besides, if your carriage should get stuck in the mud or held up by a sudden spate, what do you think would happen at Narn?"

Her sister-in-law laughed.

"A wedding without a bride would certainly be as

dismal as a wake, but perhaps the Duke would find a pretty crofter's daughter to satisfy him!"

She was being unpleasant, Clola realised, because she had not yet adjusted herself to the thought that they were to have a family relationship with the McNarns.

She was sure her sister-in-law's attitude was typical of that of many other women, whose enmity was often deeper and more violent than that of their menfolk.

Her father and brothers were waiting for her when she came downstairs, and then she saw with them a young man she had not seen before and knew that he was Torquil McNarn.

He was standing apart from her family and when she looked towards him she saw the hate in his eyes and knew that here was one of the McNarns who would not accept her so easily.

Deliberately she walked across to him.

"I regret that you and I have been unable to meet until now," she said in her soft voice, "but I hope that the poor hospitality my family have been able to offer you will not weigh against me in the future."

He was embarrassed by her attitude.

Because she had taken him by surprise, he was only able to mutter something incoherent. Then Clola turned towards her father.

"We had better get started," she said, "for I warn you, Father, I shall need quite a long time to wash and change before I set out for the Castle."

"Women!" The Kilcraig growled.

But she knew he was in too good a mood today to be disagreeable or forbidding, as he might have been on another occasion.

The warm weather, which had appeared at the beginning of July after a wet and dismal June, was unshadowed.

The sun shone out of a clear blue sky, the bees

were busy in the heather, and coveys of grouse rose ahead of them as they set off from the Castle.

"We are wasting a good shooting day," one of Clola's brother said.

"Grouse, or men?" Hamish asked irrepressibly.

They had been riding for a little over two hours when the Castle came in sight.

Clola had peeped at it often enough from the high hills on the Kilcraig land, but she had never seen it close to. Now she thought it was everything a Castle should be, an idealised structure that might have stepped out of a fairy-story.

The glen beneath it was verdant and had more trees than any glen in the Kilcraig country.

This was due to the river which ran down the centre of it, fed by burns which cascaded down the sides of the rocks.

Clola was aware that her brothers were envious, as they had no equivalent river on their land, and she wondered with a faint smile how often they had been daring enough to poach salmon here at night.

Certainly she could remember salmon on the menu when she had been a little girl, and although there would always be tales that they were brought in by one of the gillies as a tribute to their Chieftain, Clola now had her doubts.

As they drew nearer she saw crowds of men making their way up the drive which led to the Castle, and there were great numbers of what were obviously McNarn Clansmen on the skyline, blocking the road, and climbing down the sides of the cascades.

The Manse stood alone just beyond a small cluster of cottages. Beside it was the white-washed Kirk, but Clola knew that her marriage would take place in the Castle itself.

As they rode towards the Manse, the women and men who stared at them blankly and without greeting were obviously McNarns, and it was with a sense of relief that they saw how many hundreds of Kilcraigs were gathered ahead of them.

They were reclining on the ground, some sleeping or eating, while the old men were smoking their white-clay pipes.

As Clola appeared, riding beside her father, a great cry went up. Then as the Clansmen scrambled to their feet there came the roaring yell of the Kilcraig slogan.

Loud and shrill, it seemed to echo towards the Castle as they repeated it again and again.

Then in response the slogan of the McNarns came back, roar after roar. It sounded defiant, a war-cry —an exhortation to battle.

For one moment Clola looked apprehensively at her father.

Supposing instead of the peace he had envisaged the McNarns and the Kilcraigs began to fight each other in the way they had done for generations?

If this happened, if their fiery temperaments were aroused, then even their Chieftains would find it impossible to pull them apart.

But Clola had reckoned without her father's resourcefulness. He made a sign to his Piper who rode behind him, and instantly the pipes shrilled out and the noise of the slogans died away.

It was a marriage-tune he played, a tune known to every Piper and composed, it was always said, by the McCrimmonses, who were the greatest of all Pipers in Scotland.

The Kilcraig's Piper had no sooner started than he was joined by a dozen other Pipers amongst the Kilcraigs and finally by those belonging to the McNarns.

The glen swelled with their music and the hills seemed to throw back the sound so that the whole world was filled with it.

"That was clever of you, Father," Clola said as their horses came to a standstill outside the Manse door.

He smiled at her and for a moment she thought that however handsome the Duke might be, it would be impossible to admire any man more than her father for his strength, his wisdom, and his command.

The Manse door was opened and she walked inside.

The Minister's wife, a nervous, middle-aged woman, curtseyed politely and offered her food and drink before she led her upstairs to the best bed-room.

It was poorly furnished but spotlessly clean and the roses growing up the Manse wall gave the room a welcome fragrance.

The Minister's wife brought up the wedding-gown, which had been carried carefully wrapped across the back of a pony. When Clola shook it out and hung it on the outside of the wardrobe she exclaimed at the beauty of it.

Alone, Clola without hurrying took off her riding-habit, washed at the washing-stand in the corner of the room, and arranged her hair in front of the mirror.

"How are you going to dress yourself?" her sister-in-law had asked.

"I will manage," Clola replied. "I expect there will be someone who will button my gown."

"But supposing they have all gone to the Castle for the wedding?" enquired her sister-in-law, who was always ready to make difficulties.

Clola laughed.

"In that case, Father will have to do it up for me, or Hamish."

Her sister-in-law had been shocked.

"Really, Clola, you do say the most preposterous things since you have been in Edinburgh. As though any man could understand the niceties of a lady's attire!"

Clola doubted if Andrew and her younger brothers, with their preoccupation with the land, would notice if she appeared naked or wearing a sack.

But she was sure that after associating with the great beauties of London, and the women who, if rumour was to be believed, spent astronomical sums on their gowns and jewels, the Duke would be critical.

She was glad that whatever he might think of her looks, he would find it difficult to disparage her gown.

Then she wondered what he would expect her to look like.

She was aware that there would not have been time for him to learn much about her from her father, and perhaps he had not been curious.

It would have come as an overwhelming shock, she was quite certain, as it had been to her, to be forced into marrying a Kilcraig with such speed and without even a brief acquaintanceship.

"Perhaps he will be pleasantly surprised," she told herself optimistically.

Then she felt that fear, which had beset her in the night ever since she had learnt what was to happen, flow over her insidiously—fear of the unknown, fear of the man she had never met, fear of the Chief of the McNarns.

The Minister's wife came timidly back into the room to fasten her gown at the back, and exclaimed over and over again with genuine admiration at her appearance.

"Ye looks real lovely, Mistress Kilcraig," she said. "Th' bonniest bride I've ever seen! A fitting mate for th' Laird."

"Thank you," Clola replied.

"I wish ye every happiness," the elderly woman went on, and suddenly there were tears in her eyes. "Ye're so young. So young, lovely as an angel, and ye bring with ye peace te our people. God will bless ye, I know it!"

"Thank you," Clola said again.

Then on an impulse she bent and kissed the Minister's wife.

"That is to bring you luck," she said. "And thank you for your kindness."

With the tears still on her cheeks the Minister's wife escorted Clola downstairs.

Outside the Manse door was a carriage drawn by two horses.

The hood was down and as Clola stepped in she saw that behind her the procession that was to escort her to the Castle was in place.

Her brothers, with Torquil McNarn, rode behind her carriage. After them came the Bard, the Piper, The Kilcraig's special body-guard, and the senior members of the Clan, each a Chieftain in his own right on his own land.

It was impressive, but Clola had the feeling that anything they could produce would be overshadowed by the Castle and the McNarns.

The Manse was not far from the Castle drive and the road was lined with people of every age, the children holding bunches of heather in their hands, some white, some purple.

From under the fine veil of Brussels lace which covered her face Clola could look about her with curiosity, but those they passed did not cheer and anyway it would have been hard to make themselves heard above the noise of the pipes.

Now behind her father's Piper there were twelve others, all walking with a swing, wearing black cock's-tail feathers in their bonnets and blowing with crimson faces through their bone flutes.

They played two tunes before they reached the drive which led to the Castle, the carriage and horses moving slowly, at the walking pace of the procession.

Then, as they ascended the incline which led up to the Castle itself, the pipes played the march of the Kilcraigs.

It was a tune which had led them into battle for centuries, a tune which had been a challenge to the McNarns since the beginning of time.

All the way up the drive the McNarn Clansmen had stood silent and immobile as they passed. There was something a little frightening about them, and almost despite herself Clola put out her hand and slipped it into her father's.

His fingers closed over hers and she knew that whatever anyone else was feeling, he was elated at the thought that the two Clans would live in peace and the MacAuads would get their just deserts.

'I doubt if he even gave me personally a second thought,' Clola thought to herself.

She was sure of it as they reached the great iron-studded door of the Castle and there was no response from him as she relinquished his hand.

Servants in kilts sprang forward to help her alight. Then she saw waiting to receive her the tall figure of Mr. Dunblane, whom she had peeped at when he visited her father, and beside him was a small boy.

It was Jamie who came forward to say in his high, childish voice:

"Welcome on behalf of my uncle and the McNarns, Sir."

He spoke to The Kilcraig first, bowed, then bowed his small red head in Clola's direction.

"Welcome," he said.

The Kilcraig nodded perfunctorily and put out his hand to Mr. Dunblane.

Clola bent down so that her face was on a level with the boy's.

"What is your name?" she asked.

"Jamie."

"Then thank you, Jamie, for the nice way you have greeted us. I hope you and I will be friends."

"Have you brought Torquil with you?" he asked.

"He is outside."

Jamie gave a whoop of excitement.

"May I go to him?"

"Yes, I am sure you may," she answered.

He ran out through the front door and they heard him cry excitedly:

"Torquil! Torquil! You're back!"

Clola smiled at Mr. Dunblane.

"He is excited to see his brother," she said, "and it must be a relief to have Torquil home."

As she spoke, Torquil McNarn, followed by Jamie, came in through the front door.

"I ought to have been here to greet the bride," he said furiously, "but instead they brought me here tied to their chariot-wheels."

He was being angry and provocative, Clola thought, but she could understand his feelings in that he had not been allowed to go to the Castle until The Kilcraig went with him.

It was in fact insulting that her father should be afraid that the Duke would go back on his word and refuse to marry her.

Her father paid no attention to Torquil's outburst. He continued to talk to Mr. Dunblane as if nothing had happened.

"I am sorry," Clola said to Torquil in a quiet voice, "but now that you are here, will you tell us what we are to do?"

Because she seemed to need his help, the angry expression on the boy's face softened.

Assuming an air of authority, he said to Mr. Dunblane:

"Should we not get on with the ceremony? I am sure my uncle is waiting upstairs."

"Yes, of course," Mr. Dunblane replied. "Will you and Jamie lead The Kilcraig and the bride to the Chief's Room? But first you would wish to present her bouquet."

Both Torquil and Clola looked round and a servant came forward with a small bouquet of white heather tied with long satin ribbons resting on a silver salver.

Torquil took it from him and handed it to Clola with an awkward little bow.

Her father offered her his arm and they started to climb the wide, carpeted stairway which led to the first floor.

Now there was the skirl of the pipes, this time playing a wedding-march, and to the music of it Clola and The Kilcraig entered the Chief's Room.

She had a quick glimpse of an enormous and magnificent room, filled, it seemed, with men in the McNarn tartan.

Then as she moved slowly between them, peeping from beneath her long eye-lashes, she saw that the Duke was waiting for her at the far end and so was the Minister in his black robes.

After one quick glance to see if he was there, she felt too shy to raise her eyes again.

Then as her father drew her nearer and nearer she was aware of her sister-in-law and her children on the left side of the room and beside them her brothers and the senior members of the Clan.

But her eyes were drawn irresistibly to the Duke.

He looked even more splendid and more impressive wearing his rightful regalia than he did dressed as an Englishman, and she felt her heart beating with shyness and at the same time a strange excitement.

This was the man she was to marry. This was the Chieftain of a Clan larger than her father's, and a

Duke who was admired for his sportsmanship even by the English.

He was to be her husband and she was to be his wife and there would be no dividing them, for they were to be joined by God.

Now she was at the Duke's side and she looked up at him, wondering if he would be looking at her.

Then she saw that he was staring straight ahead of him at the Minister, waiting for the marriage-ceremony to begin, and there was a dark, glowering scowl on his handsome face and his lips were set in a hard, sharp line.

Chapter Four

The Duke had awakened to feel as if some menacing shadow lay over him, and his depression was not lightened as he heard the sounds of the Clansmen outside the Castle and the music from half-a-dozen different Pipers.

He realised that for his people it would be a day of excitement and rejoicing, even though they might resent their affiliation with the Kilcraigs.

But for himself, he thought, it was a day when he would walk into a trap, and there was no manner in which he could extricate himself.

He could not prevent himself from continually thinking of the woman whom he was to marry.

If ever he had visualised himself as married, it had always been to some sophisticated and beautiful creature who moved in the same world as he did. As his wife she would be admired, and even more would he be envied for his possession of her.

To know that he had no choice but to be linked with a woman of the Kilcraig family, with whom he would have nothing in common, was a horror which seemed to deepen with every second that passed.

He was quite certain that she would be barely educated, if she had had any learning at all, and would doubtless be thick-hipped and have the sturdy appearance of her menfolk.

What was more, he was afraid that his own revulsion at being forced into marriage might make it impossible to do as Lord Hinchley had suggested: give her a child and leave her as soon as possible.

Almost as if he were being taunted, he remembered all too clearly that the English always averred that it was impossible to cross the border unless one held a scented handkerchief to one's nose!

The Duke recalled how George IV when he was Prince of Wales had found that his bride, Princess Caroline, smelt unpleasant.

He had accordingly told one of her ladies-in-waiting that she was to "wash all over," but that had not prevented him from being excessively drunk on his wedding-night, which caused the marriage to founder almost before it was consummated.

The Duke was extremely fastidious where women were concerned.

He had, unlike his contemporaries, never been interested in the expensive and alluring Cyprians or "bits o' muslin" with which the Bucks of St. James's spent a great deal of their time.

Instead, his love-affairs had always been with experienced and beautiful ladies of the Beau Monde and he found it impossible to remember an instance when he had been to bed with a woman who attracted him only physically.

There had always been something else about the association that had intrigued him—her wit, her sense of humour, or perhaps only a fascinating mannerism.

Whatever it was, it raised their association from the carnal to something different.

Admittedly, such allurements palled rather quickly,

while the lady in question invariably fell deeply in love with him, finding him an ardent lover with other qualities which set him apart from the usual run of men.

This, although the Duke did not realise it, was the imagination and idealism of his Celtic blood, which was an indivisible part of his make-up.

Yet, now, by a bitter blow of fate, he was to be married to a woman he had never seen, a woman who, he was instinctively convinced, would wound not only his pride and his self-esteem but also his friends' estimation of him.

One thing the Duke swore to himself as he dressed reluctantly and with gritted teeth in the full Highland regalia that was required: he would never take his wife into Society, where his choice could be criticised.

Worse still, the marriage could be laughed at by those who at the moment respected him not only for his position and his achievements but for his good taste.

He sat down at the breakfast-table in the small Dining-Room, which was used when there was only the family present, and saw lying by his place a programme of the day's events.

He pushed it to one side, feeling that if he read it before he ate, the food would undoubtedly choke him.

Yet, when he did try to eat, he found that he was not hungry, and he ordered a glass of brandy, which was very unusual.

The Duke was far too much of an athlete to indulge in alcohol. He drank if the occasion demanded it, but even then sparingly, and his choice in his own house in the South was invariably champagne or good French claret.

He had not brought these North with him, relying on

his father's cellars, but he had included in his luggage some kegs of excellent brandy.

He thought as he sipped it slowly that it would steady his nerves and make it easier to face the ordeal that lay ahead.

It was early, and the marriage-ceremony was the first item on the agenda. This was to be completed as quickly as possible because so much time would be taken up in accepting the allegiance of the Clansmen.

The Duke was just about to rise from the breakfast-table when Lord Hinchley joined him, saying:

"The noise outside, which sounds like Bartholomew Fair, makes it impossible for me to sleep, Taran, so I have risen at this unearthly hour."

He looked at the expression on the Duke's face and added:

"Perhaps it is a good thing, because now I am here to cheer you up."

"Nothing could do that," the Duke replied.

"Quite frankly, I am very sorry for you," Lord Hinchley answered, "but, as there is nothing you can do to avoid it, you must make the best of a bad job."

Lord Hinchley sat down at the breakfast-table, and when the servants, having helped him, had left the room, he said:

"Take my advice. Cut your losses and come to Edinburgh as quickly as possibly. I must leave here the day after tomorrow."

"So soon?" the Duke murmured automatically.

"Soon?" Lord Hinchley exclaimed. "I have stayed, at your special request, for your wedding for longer than I had intended, but I thought we might have one more day's shooting. I have never known grouse to be more plentiful. But then I really must be about my duties."

"I do realise it would be impossible for you to arrive after the King," the Duke joked, and Lord Hinchley gave an exclamation of horror.

"God forbid! I should be shot at dawn, incarcerated in the Tower, or, worse still, confined in the dungeons of Edinburgh Castle!"

"That, I admit, would be the ultimate punishment," the Duke said sourly.

"Then join me in Edinburgh. I presume you will be going by sea?"

"It is quicker," the Duke replied, "and I believe Dunblane has already sent off our Clansmen who are to represent the McNarn Yeomen at the Review on Portobello Sands, but they, of course, are riding to Edinburgh."

"I see you are really becoming a Scot," Lord Hinchley said. "At least in appearance."

The Duke gave a sigh that was curiously like a groan, and because his friend was really sorry for the predicament in which he found himself he changed the subject.

All too soon, it seemed to the Duke, it was time for them both to repair to the Chief's Room, where the marriage-ceremony was to take place.

As space was naturally limited, only relatives and the most important personages of the two Clans were invited inside the Castle.

The Duke and Lord Hinchley entered the Chief's Room when everyone else including the Minister was already there.

In the few minutes that the Duke had to wait he had time to notice The Kilcraig's relations and recognise his eldest son, Andrew, and beside him his wife.

One look at her told him all too clearly the type of woman he was being forced to marry.

Mrs. Andrew Kilcraig had a pleasant face but had lost her figure bearing three children.

Dressed plainly in a manner which made the Duke

think that if he had seen her in London he would have mistaken her for a servant-girl, her skin was tanned by the sun and her hair was the pale sandy shade of red that had nothing to recommend it as a feminine adornment.

The Duke looked at her and then looked away.

He had always disliked red hair, whether it was the red portrayed by Titian and so much admired on the Continent or was the more flamboyant red associated with many Scottish women.

Once again he felt everything that was fastidious in him recoil in horror at what lay ahead.

He thought of what the Prince of Wales had had to put up with through Princess Caroline's unclean habits.

The Duke modelled himself, as soon as he had been old enough, on the strict principle of cleanliness which had been laid down for the Beaux and Dandies by Beau Brummell.

Brummell had been so obsessed that he had even had the soles of his shoes polished, and had sent his linen to be washed in Hampstead, which, he averred, made it smell of sweet country air.

Frenchmen who worked to copy his elegance had their own dirty linen sent across the Channel to be washed by English laundresses and laid out in the sun on Hampstead Heath.

The Prince of Wales had in fact at the beginning of the century swept away the uncleanliness of the generation before him.

Only a few of his older associates, like Charles James Fox and the Duke of Norfolk, wore dirty linen and apparently washed as infrequently as possible.

The Duke insisted on a cleanliness in his own houses which echoed that of Carlton House, and, when the Regent succeeded to the Monarchy, of Buckingham Palace and Windsor Castle.

Now he thought that if his wife was dirty as well as

unprepossessing it would be impossible to follow Lord Hinchley's advice or even to touch her.

'She can stay here,' he thought savagely to himself, 'and rot, for all I care!'

He heard the swirl of the bag-pipes and knew that the moment was upon him. Then, as he was aware that The Kilcraig was coming down the centre of the room with the bride on his arm, he knew he could not look.

It was not only cowardice, it was a feeling of being unable to come face to face with the destruction of his pride and the foundation on which he believed his life was built.

He therefore stood staring ahead, and as the Minister in his broad Scottish accent started the Service he found it impossible to listen to the words, conscious only of his own feelings of rebellion and anger.

For the first time, it struck him that his father had won.

He had imagined when he ran away that he had escaped him and was free not only of the brutality of the parent he had loathed but of all the hide-bound customs and superstitions that were embodied in the Castle.

It had been to him a place of torment, while the people who lived there were his natural enemies, because they gave their loyalty to his father.

Now that he had come back, his father had recaptured him and he had become a prisoner of everything from which he believed he had escaped.

The Minister's voice droned on, then the Duke was aware that Lord Hinchley was handing him a wedding-ring.

He put it onto a finger that seemed to appear from out of a white mist and steeled himself against revulsion at his first contact with the woman who was now his wife.

Then the Minister said the last prayer over them and it was with a sense of relief that the Duke could move. Although he had given his arm to his Duchess, he did not look at her.

It had been arranged by Mr. Dunblane that they should all repair to the large Dining-Hall for a wedding-breakfast.

This would entail, the Duke was aware, a meal of gigantic proportions, consisting mostly of a profusion of meats which had been in preparation since the day they had left Kilcraig Castle with no choice but to accept the ultimatum.

Everyone who had attended the ceremony in the Chief's Room could be seated in the Baronial Dining-Hall, which had been added to the Castle by William Adam and was a magnificent example of that great architect's work.

The carved ceiling, painted and gilded, was a treasure in itself, and the huge mantelpiece, of Italian stone carved by craftsmen who had been brought especially to Scotland by his grandfather, was unique.

The furniture was as outstanding as the paintings.

To the Duke it was all very familiar, but to Clola it was a surprise and a delight that she had not expected.

She thought that the Castle would be fine but she had not thought to find it filled with treasures that she had learnt and read about in Edinburgh but never expected to see in her own land.

Vaguely at the back of her mind she remembered hearing that the Duke's grandfather had been a great traveller.

It must have been he, she thought, who had brought so many fine foreign paintings to the Castle and perhaps too the French furniture, which she had noted in the corridors as they moved through them.

Sitting next to the Duke at the top of the long table at which were seated many of the kinfolk of the Kilcraigs as well as those of the McNarns, Clola was glad that the Duke did not speak to her.

She knew that if he did so it would cost him a tremendous effort, for she had felt his anger emanating from him as they had stood side by side before the Minister. She had known even more intimately what he was feeling when his fingers had touched hers in the giving of the ring.

'He hates me!' she had thought.

While it frightened and perturbed her, she thought that perhaps if they could talk alone together it would be easier than if he faced her with enmity in public.

She therefore bent her head so that the lace veil which had been flung back after the wedding-ceremony fell like a curtain on either side of her face.

She knew that such a gesture would be attributed to the shyness which was expected of a bride, and no-one was likely to comment on it.

She, like the Duke, could force herself to eat only very little of the many dishes that were laid before them, and she was glad too that because of the strenuousness of the afternoon ahead there were to be no speeches.

The toast to their health was proposed by The Kilcraig in just a few short words.

She was not aware that the Duke had said to Mr. Dunblane when he had wished to discuss the details of the wedding:

"Arrange anything you like. If I have to be a performer in this circus I will do what is expected of me and no more!"

Finally he had said to his Comptroller:

"What is more, I will not make a speech, nor will I listen to any. Make any excuse you like, or tell the truth. I have been blackmailed into this marriage and I shall not pretend to enjoy it!"

"I will try to make everything as painless as possible, Your Grace," Mr. Dunblane promised.

"Dammit, Dunblane! How could this have happened to me?" the Duke asked.

For a moment Mr. Dunblane thought it was the same cry that he had heard from the Duke twelve years ago when as a boy he had said in almost the same voice:

"How can I endure this any longer? It is impossible!"

Young Taran had in fact broken under the strain and run away to freedom. But he had come back to find himself embroiled, through no fault of his own, in a situation about which anyone must feel sympathetic.

And yet, Mr. Dunblane thought philosophically, good might come out of evil.

He had, although he would not admit it to the Duke, an enormous respect for The Kilcraig.

He was a great Chieftain, the old-fashioned type who had made the Clans at one time small armies within themselves, following a code of honour and an integrity that if it had been known universally would have been admired by the entire world.

The word "Clan" means "Children." The Kilcraig and his like considered themselves the fathers of their families, loved and feared, benevolent at their best and exercising their terrifying power of "pit and gallows" at their worst.

The Kilcraig Clan's excessive pride came from a belief in a common ancestry and an exclusive identity that placed them above other races and especially the men of the South.

It was this pride which made them fight with a courage and a valour that was the terror of other armies and was to earn them later the name of "The Devils in Petticoats."

In Gaelic terms, Mr. Dunblane knew, killing and

death was always heroic and grief was its shining laurel for the slain.

Somewhere between the vision and the reality there were men like The Kilcraig, struggling to lead his people and to do what was best for them.

'If the Duke will only stay with us, he too will be a great Chieftain!' Mr. Dunblane thought, but he was well aware that there was a very large question-mark over the Duke's immediate plans.

At last, when the Duke had begun to think that time was standing still, the meal came to an end and in traditional manner the Piper played round the table, stopping beside the Duke's chair to receive a word of appreciation and a small silver cup filled with whisky.

He said the Gaelic word *Slainte*, which means "Health," drank it in one draught, and was then ready to lead the Duke from the Banqueting-Hall along the corridors and out through the front door to the front of the Castle.

Again without looking at her the Duke offered his arm to Clola, and as they appeared on the steps of the Castle a great cry went up which seemed to shake the very turrets.

It was the slogan of the Kilcraigs and that of the McNarns yelled at the same time by hundreds of men, deafeningly explosive, and yet at the same time evoking in those who heard it a pride that was unmistakable.

Without pausing, his Piper leading the way, the Duke and Duchess walked from the door of the Castle towards the place where all the Chieftains of the McNarn Clan had in the past accepted the homage of their Clansmen.

There were stories of how the Kings of Scotland had met there and tales, believed by the Clansmen, that the Kings' ghosts could still be seen and their places sometimes taken by the giants and monsters who lived high in the mountains.

But today there was only one chair, which had been fashioned from the antlers of stags, every one of them a Royal.

The chair had been made for the first Earl of Strathnarn, whose title had been created after a battle in which his Clansmen had distinguished themselves with conspicuous gallantry.

The Duke stood in front of the chair, The Kilcraig standing beside him, and Mr. Dunblane handed him a dirk.

First The Kilcraig kissed the metal of which it was fashioned, then said in a voice which rang out so that all the Clansmen who were listening could hear:

"On this drawn dirk I take my oath to extend the hand of friendship to the Chief of the McNarns. The feuds of the past are forgotten and we will face the future as brothers, commanding all those who follow us to do likewise. On this I swear, and if I ever prove perjured may I be stabbed with this same weapon for having betrayed my trust."

He kissed the blade again and handed it to the Duke, who repeated the same oath before handing the dirk back to Mr. Dunblane.

Then the two Chieftains clasped their hands together and bowed to each other. Another chair was set with that of the Duke's and he and The Kilcraig sat down side by side.

Then The Kilcraig said in a loud voice:

"The Oath of Allegiance will be given by our followers to us both, but first, My Lord Duke, your wife—my daughter—will swear allegiance to you."

The Duke drew in his breath.

Now he knew he would have to look at the woman he had married, touch her hand, and kiss her cheeks.

It was the Oath of Allegiance that had always

been given in the past to the Kings of Scotland, and he wondered if any King had ever been as reluctant as he was to accept it.

Then as she moved in front of him the first thing he noticed was that her gown was not only in the height of fashion but very elegant, and that she moved with a grace that he had not expected.

For the first time since the wedding-ceremony Clola held her head high on her long neck in a way that had commanded a great deal of admiration in Edinburgh.

For a moment she stood facing the Duke and he saw in astonishment not the homely Scottish woman he had expected but someone so beautiful, and yet so unusual, that he thought he must have imagined her.

There was no doubt that Clola was lovely, and her dark hair was in contrast to her white skin, which had the texture of a magnolia.

Her eyes were dark but with touches of gold in them like the sunlight on a stream, framed by a fringe of lashes that curled back like a child's.

They seemed to hold in their depths a mystery which was part of the Castle towering above them and the high mountains in the distance.

For the first time it struck the Duke that her voice when she repeated the marriage-vows had been very soft and musical, and he knew before he touched them that her hands too would be soft and sensitive.

For a moment they stared at each other as if they had forgotten they were being watched by hundreds of curious eyes. Then with the grace of a swan Clola went down on her knees in front of the Duke.

Slowly and distinctly she said the ancient words of the Oath of Allegiance:

"So may God help me as I shall support Thee. I swear and hold up my hand to obey, defend, and

serve Thee as long as my life lasts and if needs to be die for Thee."

Her hands were outstretched in front of her, palms together, pointing upwards in an attitude of prayer.

The Duke covered them with his own and accepted her allegiance, then bent his head formally and kissed her first on one cheek, then the other.

As he did so he felt her fingers tremble in his and there was a faint fragrance of a French perfume that he did not recognise, and then the ceremony was over.

He rose and helped Clola to her feet, then as he looked round as if to find a chair for her she shook her head and moved as she had been told to stand beside his chair.

It seemed discourteous but the Duke suspected that by custom only he and The Kilcraig as head of the Clans could sit in this traditional place.

Then he had no time to think of anything else, for the Chiefs came forward one after another to kneel on one knee in front of him and The Kilcraig and swear their allegiance.

Clola had taken the oath in English, while the Clansmen spoke in Gaelic.

The Duke was not aware that Clola, after watching and listening to the Clansmen for some time, had been taken back to the Castle by Mr. Dunblane.

"You must be tired, Your Grace," he said as he drew her away and they walked side by side over the grass towards the front door.

"I am, a little," Clola admitted. "I think it is because I found it difficult to sleep last night, and we rose very early to reach here."

"I do not need to tell you," Mr. Dunblane said, "that you are the most beautiful bride anyone could hope to see, whatever their Clan might be."

"I am more afraid of the criticism of the McNarns

than the admiration of the Kilcraigs!" Clola laughed.

"I do not think you need be afraid of anything," Mr. Dunblane replied.

He had in fact been astounded by Clola's beauty as she came into the Chief's Room on the arm of her father.

Then he thought that perhaps when her veil was raised there would be flaws in the face beneath it. But instead he knew, watching her in the Banqueting-Hall, that she was in fact the loveliest person he had ever seen.

How could The Kilcraig have bred anything so exquisite and kept it a secret? he wondered.

He was curious but delighted in a manner he had never expected—for here was the answer to the question of whether the Duke would stay in Scotland.

Only Mr. Dunblane was aware of how important to the McNarns was their Chieftain for the life of the Clan.

He had thought when the old Duke died that it would be impossible for anyone to take his place or to keep up the high standard of behaviour that had been shown by the McNarns during his lifetime.

And yet when he saw the new Duke he had known that here was another man in whom the Clansmen would be able to put their trust.

Mr. Dunblane, who was very intelligent, was a Scot who loved his country with a passion that made it agonising for him to know how Clans bereft of their Chieftain deteriorated and to learn the tragedy of what was happening in Sutherland.

But while he was a patriot he was also an extremely practical man.

He had friends who had told him a great deal about the activities of the Marquis of Narn.

He knew about his sporting achievements, his friendship with the King, and his position as leader amongst the Courtiers and those who were admitted to the Royal Circle.

This was the life in which the new Duke had won for himself the most distinguished place, but there was another one waiting for him: one in which if he liked he could be King, not Courtier—first, not second.

Mr. Dunblane looked at Clola now and thought she embodied all the legends sung or recited of snow-maidens and wild nymphs, and he wondered if the Duke would think the same.

They reached the Castle and he took her up the staircase and into a very elegant Drawing-Room where the walls were of blue brocade, the furniture was French, and there were huge vases of flowers on many of the polished tables.

"This is always known as the Duchess's Room," Mr. Dunblane explained, "and I thought perhaps you would wish to say good-bye to your family here before they return home."

"Perhaps you would tell my sister-in-law where I am, and she could join me," Clola suggested.

"I will do that," Mr. Dunblane said, "but I thought first I would show you your bed-room, which is on this floor."

He led Clola down a long corridor and she could see that the walls were of great thickness and this part of the Castle had been built as an impregnable stronghold against enemies.

Mr. Dunblane opened a door and Clola followed him into a room which looked out on the other side of the Castle.

Here was a more magnificent view than she had expected, over the moorlands to where there was a great loch fringed by high hills.

The room had a painted ceiling rioting with gods and goddesses and cupids, and there was a huge four-poster bed hung with satin curtains. The furniture was French, as was the carpet.

"I never expected to find anything so lovely!" Clola exclaimed.

"This has been the Duchess's bed-room for centuries," Mr. Dunblane explained. "It is in the old part of the Castle but was redecorated by the last Duke, as was the Chieftain's Room next door."

A faint flush came to Clola's cheeks and Mr. Dunblane said quickly:

"I will find your sister-in-law and bring her to the Duchess's Room."

"Thank you, you have been very kind," Clola said. "When I watched you behind the curtains of the window arriving at my home, I did hope that one day I would meet you."

"I pray, Duchess, that we shall be friends and that I can help you if you need help."

"I am quite sure that I shall need not only help but also a friend," Clola replied.

She held out her hand as she spoke and Mr. Dunblane took it in his, then raised it to his lips.

"It is difficult for me to find words," he said, "in which to tell you how glad I am that you are here."

There was a ring of sincerity in his voice which warmed Clola, and when she was alone she stood for a moment looking at the door through which he had passed, then at the furnishings of the bed-room.

"There is so much to see," she murmured to herself.

She would have liked to take off her wedding-veil, but she did not know if she would be required to appear again, in which case it would be a great mistake to change her appearance.

Perhaps she and the Duke would have to walk amongst the Clansmen and talk to their wives. She did not know, and she wished she had asked Mr. Dunblane before he had left her.

Interested in everything she saw, she moved back to the Duchess's Room and give a little exclamation of delight as she found that on one wall there was a built-in bookcase containing many books which she knew she would enjoy reading.

She was joined, as Mr. Dunblane had promised, very shortly by her sister-in-law and her children.

One small boy was about the same age as Jamie and almost as soon as they were brought into the room they disappeared together, as Jamie said he had something to show his new friend.

"This is certainly far grander than I expected," Mrs. Andrew Kilcraig said, looking round with an air that told Clola she would like to find fault.

Clola did not answer and after a moment she went on:

"I suppose you realise how lucky you are? You may have been forced into marrying a McNarn, but after all he is very presentable and apparently has plenty of money!"

"I have been told little about my husband," Clola said in her soft voice.

"I expect you will learn all you have to soon enough," her sister-in-law said tartly. "Well, I have only come to say good-bye. As it is we shall be back long after the children's bed-time, and they will be as cross as two sticks, if I know anything about them!"

Clola was not sorry to see her go, and the only delay was that they could not find Jamie and Andrew's son and the servants hunted all over the Castle before finally they were discovered on the roof.

"We had a wonderful view, Mama," the young Kilcraig said.

"View or no view, you had no right to disappear!"

his mother snapped. "I shall tell your grandfather how badly you have behaved when we get home!"

Clola thought with a smile that this was the ultimate threat at Kilcraig Castle, but when her sister-in-law and the children had driven off she felt lonely.

Although she was a bride and this was her wedding-day it seemed that no-one wanted her, and she wondered how soon it would be before she and the Duke were alone.

There was in fact no chance of that before dinner-time.

Mr. Dunblane came to tell Clola that the oaths of allegiance were taking far longer than they had anticipated.

"I could not have believed that so many Clansmen would reach here in such a short time," he said, "and I suppose it is my fault for underestimating the number. Anyway, I will take the blame."

"So, what is to happen?" Clola asked.

"I have arranged for dinner at seven o'clock, and your father will eat with you before he starts on the journey home."

"He will be very late," Clola said.

"It will not be dark," Mr. Dunblane replied.

"No, not really dark," Clola agreed.

"Your brothers, of course, will dine at the same time," Mr. Dunblane went on. "I expect you would like to bathe and to change your gown. Your luggage should all have been unpacked for you by now."

"That sounds delightful!" Clola exclaimed with a smile.

"I have arranged for Mrs. Forse, who is quite intelligent, to look after you," Mr. Dunblane said. "Later, of course, we will find you a personal lady's-maid—perhaps a woman from Edinburgh. But Mrs. Forse will, I am sure, be able to do all that you require of her for the moment."

"I am sure she will," Clola answered. "And thank you for all the arrangements you have made for me."

"Let me assure you that it is a very great pleasure!" Mr. Dunblane smiled. "And now may I escort you to your room?"

Clola put down the book she had been reading.

"I can find my own way to my bed-room," she said. "I know how busy you must be."

"Then we will meet at dinner," Mr. Dunblane said, "and I will arrange for everyone to gather here so that it will not seem so formal as in the Chief's Room."

"Thank you," Clola said again.

She felt quite light-hearted as she walked towards her bed-room. After all, with Mr. Dunblane at the Castle it did not seem so frightening as it had at first.

She walked into her room.

A middle-aged woman was arranging Clola's hair-brushes on the dressing-table.

She turned as Clola entered and dropped a curtsey.

"You must be Mrs. Forse," Clola said, moving towards her and holding out her hand.

To her surprise, the woman ignored it.

"That's ma name, Yer Grace."

"Mr. Dunblane tells me that you will look after me until I can obtain a personal maid."

"Them are ma orders, Yer Grace."

She spoke in a quiet, restrained voice which somehow sounded unnatural.

Then, when she raised her eyes, Clola knew why, for she saw an expression of such hatred that she recoiled from it as if she had found a serpent on her path.

Quite unaccountably, she found her heart beating in a manner which told her she was afraid.

'I am being stupid. It is just because I am over-tired,' she thought; and aloud she said:

"Forse is an unusual name. Do you come from this part of the world?"

"I'm a McNarn," the woman replied fiercely. "A McNarn, Yer Grace, born an' bred."

Clola did not say anything, but as if she felt she must give an explanation Mrs. Forse went on:

"Me husband were called Forse. He came from Caithness, an' a great mistake I made in marrying out o' the Clan. He left me wi' a child ta bring up on ma own, so I came back ta ma ain people."

"I am sorry," Clola said.

She felt the woman spoke in a manner which made her sound as though she was slightly unhinged.

It seemed as if, having spoken, Mrs. Forse had nothing more to say.

Almost in silence, except when she had to question Clola as to her choice of dress, she assisted her to undress, poured water into the bath that was arranged in a small room off the bed-room, and buttoned Clola into her evening-gown.

She had chosen one of pale pink which her grandmother had bought for her at the same time as the one which she had worn for her wedding.

It had been very expensive, and her grandmother had envisaged her wearing it, with the addition of a train, at the Reception that was to be held in the Drawing-Room at Holyrood Palace when the King would meet the most distinguished ladies of Scotland.

'It is far more important that I should look attractive tonight,' Clola thought to herself, 'for it is not the King I have to please, but my husband.'

She knew, and it would have been foolish to pretend otherwise, that she was looking her best; in fact, those who had admired her in Edinburgh certainly would have said that she was looking her most beautiful as she left her bed-room to go to the Duchess's Room.

"Thank you, Mrs. Forse," she said as the Scottish woman opened the door for her.

Mrs. Forse did not reply. She only looked at Clola with that expression in her eyes which made her shiver.

Dinner was delicious, with dishes which were cooked with a delicacy that had not been apparent at the Wedding-Breakfast.

Clola realised that everyone was very tired, including her father and the Duke.

It had been a long day, and although The Kilcraig talked of what they had achieved, it was obvious that he was in a hurry to start on his journey home.

She was aware that Lord Hinchley was looking at her in a bemused fashion, but she found it hard to keep her own eyes from the Duke's face.

She felt that he was no longer angry as he had been at the wedding-ceremony, and yet she was not sure.

She only knew that she felt shy and now the fears that had beset her last night and this morning were back.

When dinner was over there were farewells to take of her own family, and as Clola saw them off she was aware of the noise coming from the Clansmen.

She had a suspicion that a great number of them were getting drunk, which was not surprising as she had realised that there had been plenty of ale, provided by the Duke, with which they could celebrate.

There was the smell of roasting oxen, lamb, and stag, and in the dusk there was the light of fires being kindled over the moorlands opposite the Castle and in the valley beneath them.

There was also the skirl of the bag-pipes, the cries of those who were dancing reels, and voices singing and sudden bursts of somewhat intoxicated laughter.

"They are certainly enjoying themselves!" Lord Hinchley said as The Kilcraig rode away and they turned back to enter the Castle.

Clola had noticed that Torquil ran for a little while beside Hamish's pony, obviously unwilling to break off a conversation they were having.

Then he joined them as they all walked up the stairs together.

"That was a jolly good wedding, Uncle Taran!" he said.

The Duke turned to look at him as he said:

"I wish to speak to you, Torquil!"

There was an ominous note in his tone and Clola longed to cry out:

"Not tonight! Do not say it tonight, on top of all the other things that have happened today."

She looked at Torquil's paling face, and then almost pleadingly at Lord Hinchley.

He seemed not to understand that she was appealing to him, and he said to the Duke:

"Shall the Duchess and I wait for you in the Sitting-Room?"

"No!" the Duke replied unexpectedly. "I want her to come with me."

He walked ahead to the Chief's Room and Clola and Torquil followed him. When the door was shut behind them the Duke said:

"Your family took my nephew prisoner, and doubtless they will ask you what punishment I have given him for his behaviour which has resulted in several unforeseen consequences."

Clola winced, as she knew he was referring to their marriage.

Looking at Torquil, the Duke said:

"It is your behaviour which brought me here from the South and because of it I have married a Kilcraig. What may be the result of that is a question that only the future can decide. But now I have to say this. . . ."

He paused for a moment and Clola saw Torquil brace himself as if for a blow.

"As you are aware," the Duke went on, "I am forced to leave for Edinburgh within the next day or so to meet the King when he arrives, and to lead the Clan at a Review which has been commanded by His Majesty."

Torquil nodded, indicating that he was aware of that, and the Duke continued:

"While I am in Edinburgh I intend to arrange for you to go to school there for a year. After that time, if you have learnt enough—and that will certainly mean a great deal of hard work—I will send you to Oxford."

Torquil's eyes widened for a moment in astonishment, then he stammered almost beneath his breath:

"O-Oxford?"

"I hope you will enjoy it as much as I did, and when you are South you will doubtless have the opportunity of going abroad and visiting France, Italy, and perhaps Greece."

Clola could see that Torquil was absolutely stunned, but when he did not speak the Duke continued:

"Those are the plans I have made for you and which Mr. Dunblane agrees would be in your best interests, but I must also give you a warning."

Now the Duke's voice changed and he said sternly:

"If before the beginning of the school term you get into mischief of any sort, if you behave with stupidity and a lack of responsibility, then I shall send you to a school in Glasgow which I understand caters to boys who need restraint and discipline. Do I make myself clear?"

"You do indeed, Uncle Taran!" Torquil cried. "I never thought I had a hope of going to Oxford! Thank you, thank you, Sir!"

"You had better go and thank Mr. Dunblane," the Duke said. "Perhaps we had both better go; I imagine there are quite a lot of things he will want to tell you about your future."

The Duke walked towards the door, but Torquil reached it before him and held it open, and then they both waited for Clola. She smiled at the Duke a little shyly as she passed him. Then, because she thought it was expected of her, she went to the Duchess's Room.

Lord Hinchley, who was looking at a newspaper, rose to his feet.

"You are still in one piece?" he asked. "I thought Taran sounded rather like my School-Master when he was going to beat me!"

"He has been very kind to his nephew," Clola replied, "and Torquil is thrilled at the idea of going to Oxford."

"I've always thought that Taran's bark was worse than his bite!" Lord Hinchley smiled. "After all, he was the same age as young Torquil when he ran away from home, so he ought to have a kindred feeling for him."

Clola sat down on the sofa and Lord Hinchley stared at her for a moment. Then he said:

"You are very beautiful! How could I imagine that anything so lovely would be languishing here in the Highlands?"

Clola smiled.

This was the second man today who had called her beautiful, and she wondered with a little feeling of excitement if the third would be her husband.

But whatever the Duke had to say to Mr. Dunblane and Torquil, it certainly took a long time.

When the clock on the mantelpiece struck a half-after-ten and the Duke still had not returned, Clola rose to her feet.

"If you will forgive me, I think I will retire," she said to Lord Hinchley. "It has been a long and exciting day."

"I can understand that," Lord Hinchley said, "but I hate to let you go. There is so much more I would like to talk to you about."

Clola smiled.

Lord Hinchley had done all the talking and she realised that he wanted to show off, to tell her what a close friend he was of the Duke's, and to make sure that she too would accept him as a friend.

She gave him her hand, and just as Mr. Dunblane had done, he kissed it, and then she went along to her own bed-room.

She was not certain what her feelings were when she entered the room.

She found Mrs. Forse waiting for her and once again she had an intimation not only of hatred but of evil.

But she was too tired to trouble herself over the woman, and she let her help her to undress in silence.

Then, when she was in her nightgown and just about to get into bed, Mrs. Forse said:

"This is yer weddin'-nicht, Yer Grace, a nicht when we should be wishin' ye great happiness, but I wish ye nothin' o' the kind!"

"Then it would be best if you just said good-night, Mrs. Forse," Clola said with dignity.

"I'll no wish ye guid-nicht. It can be nothing but bad. Bad for His Grace and bad for the McNarns that they should link with the Kilcraigs, who have the stains o' our blood upon their hands!"

The woman spoke with such ferocity that Clola wished she did not feel it difficult to silence her, or to drive her from the room when she was only wearing a thin, diaphanous, lace-trimmed nightgown.

"I do not wish to hear that sort of talk, Mrs. Forse," she managed to say sharply. "My father, as you well know, has sworn the oath of friendship and loyalty to the McNarns and the Duke has sworn the same to the

Kilcraigs. There will be no more talk of bloodshed or enmity between us."

"That's what ye may believe, Yer Grace, but the spirits o' the dead will not be appeased by worrds. They cry oot for vengeance!"

Mrs. Forse's voice seemed to echo evilly round the room. Then she walked towards the door.

"It's been a bad day, Yer Grace," she said as she reached it. "A bad day an' an evil day! But retribution will come! Ye can be sure o' that. There'll be retribution, an' 'tis upon yer head that it'll fall!"

As she spoke the last word she closed the door and there was a silence in which Clola could hear her heart beating.

Chapter Five

Clola stood staring at the door which Mrs. Forse had closed behind her, and as she turned to look towards the great bed she was suddenly afraid.

Afraid of the hatred which the Housekeeper had spat at her, and afraid of the hatred she had felt emanating from the Duke during the wedding-ceremony.

It seemed to be closing in on her and she was aware that in what had always been the enemy's camp she was alone, far from her own family and everything that was familiar.

She had a longing to be with those who bore her name, who were outside celebrating what she felt would be a "mockery of a marriage."

Without really thinking, carried by an impulse that was stronger than thought, she opened the door of her bed-room and crossed the wide corridor, trying to find another room which would look out on the front of the Castle where the Kilcraigs were encamped.

She opened the first door she came to, and, though it was unlit by candles, the light from the windows told her she was seeing the glow from the fires that had been lit below the Castle.

Shutting the door quietly behind her, she crossed the room, feeling that the golden light drew her and she must run to it for safety.

When she reached the window she could see, as she had expected, dozens of small fires round which the Clansmen were sitting and several big ones where she knew they would be roasting meat.

Now the comforting sound of the pipes was in her ears and she stood there wishing desperately that she could be amongst those whom she knew rather than incarcerated in a place where there was nothing but hatred.

She felt panic-stricken at the thought of what lay ahead of her.

It had been strange enough to come home, after three years, from the life she had lived in Edinburgh with her grandmother.

Because she was so acutely sensitive, it had been hard at first to adjust herself and not let her father and brothers know that there was any need for adjustment.

But this step into the unknown aroused a fear that was almost a terror.

How could she live with a man who hated her, and with servants like Mrs. Forse crying out for the vengeance of the dead? And, Clola knew, they believed every word they said.

She had thought it would be difficult to live at her father's Castle, without the intelligent people, the music, and the books which had all been so much a part of her life in Edinburgh.

But at least she had belonged there, at least she was part of a family, while here . . .

She felt herself trembling, and her heart, which had beaten frantically when Mrs. Forse had raged at her, was still thumping in her breast, sounding almost like the beat of doom.

"I cannot . . . bear it! I must go . . . away! I must . . . hide somewhere!" Clola said frantically.

Then in the darkness of the room behind her she was aware of a "presence."

She knew it was not human, yet it was very real.

She sensed it as she had sensed so often things that other people could not see or hear, and yet to her they were present.

She felt it come nearer and yet she was unafraid; she knew it was a Lady, grey and insubstantial, who understood what she was feeling and reached out to her from the World Beyond.

The feeling of the Lady's presence was so vivid that Clola felt she could almost hear the words of comfort she spoke.

"You must be brave and unafraid," the Lady told her.

"How . . . how can . . . I?" Clola asked.

"Fate has sent you. There are things to be done which only you can do."

Like a child who has run to his mother for safety, Clola felt her agitation subsiding. Then, as the violent beating of her heart abated and she no longer trembled, she felt calmer but desperately tired.

Almost as if the Grey Lady beside her took her by the hand, she walked blindly to the bed, seeing its shadowy outline in the light from the window.

It was not made up with sheets, but beneath the velvet cover there were blankets and pillows.

Clola felt that the Grey Lady helped her onto the blankets and pulled the velvet cover over her.

Then as her head touched the pillow she fell asleep to the music of the pipes.

* * *

Clola awoke with a start to find the sunshine coming through two long windows. At first she wondered where she was, and then she remembered.

She sat up, realising that she had slept all night in a bed without sheets, but it had been warm and comfortable under the cover, which had been embroidered by loving hands.

It was quiet and she thought that by now the Clansmen would be dispersing back to their homes and the work which would be waiting for them.

She looked round and saw that the room was panelled and that the curtains and the hangings of the bed were embroidered with seventeenth-century needlework.

It was an austere room compared with the furnishings in the rest of the Castle, and she thought that as it was in the old part of the building it must have changed very little through the passing centuries, even though it had been redecorated by the late Duke.

She slipped out of bed and went to the window. As she had expected, most of the Clansmen had gone and there was no Kilcraig tartan to be seen amongst those tidying up the debris left from the night before.

She wondered if she had dreamt the presence of the Grey Lady who had come to her aid when she had been so afraid. Then she was sure that the Lady was real, as real as those moving about below, and the other people in the Castle, and even Clola herself.

She was about to turn towards the door when she saw over the mantelpiece a portrait. It was very old, painted on wood, and enclosed in an ancient carved frame.

Looking at it, Clola knew without being told that here was the Lady who had come to her rescue.

She moved nearer and looked at the inscription under the portrait.

Morag, 3rd Countess of Strathnarn
1488–1548

Looking at the portrait, Clola could see a serene face, not beautiful but with something spiritual and wise about it.

Here, then, was her Grey Lady. Here was someone who must in her lifetime have helped those in need and still extended her help beyond the grave.

"Thank you," Clola said quietly, and went to her bed-room.

Because she had no wish to see Mrs. Forse until she had to, she did not ring the bell, but washed in cold water and then dressed herself in one of the attractive gowns which her grandmother had bought for her in Edinburgh.

When she was ready to leave her room she looked rather fearfully at the door which she knew led into the Duke's bed-room.

Had he come to her last night and found her gone? Or had he hated her so violently that the door had remained closed?

She remembered how his eyes had met hers before she made the Oath of Allegiance before him. She had felt then that in some way they spoke to each other without words.

Later she was sure she had been mistaken and he must still have been hating her as he had hated her in the Chief's Room, where they were married.

If he had come to her last night, would he have thought that she was breaking her oath to obey and serve him as she had promised to do?

With a deep sigh Clola thought that while the Grey Lady had brought her peace and rest during the night, the problems were still there.

And yet, because she was rested, they were not so

fearful and she felt somehow that she could cope with them.

She looked at the clock and saw that she had taken longer in dressing than she had intended and it was in fact nearly half-after-eight.

'I will go down to breakfast,' she thought, 'and I shall know by the Duke's expression if he is still angry with me or not.'

She walked along the corridor and encountered Mrs. Forse, obviously coming to her room, carrying a tray which held tea-things.

She looked surprised when she saw Clola, who merely inclined her head as she passed, saying: "Good-morning, Mrs. Forse!"

It was too early, she thought, for dramatics, curses, or threats of vengeance, and the less conversation she had with Mrs. Forse the better!

She remembered how Mr. Dunblane had said that she could have a personal maid of her own, and she decided that she would speak to him as soon as possible and ask for one to be provided.

She entered the Dining-Room to find only Jamie, eating alone, and she said:

"Good-morning, Jamie!"

"Good-morning," Jamie replied. "Everyone's gone shooting, but they wouldn't take me."

"Everyone except me!" came a voice from the door.

Torquil came in as he spoke to throw himself down in a chair at the table without greeting Clola.

The servants set a bowl of porridge in front of her and one in front of Torquil.

"It's jolly unfair!" he said, speaking to nobody in particular and not looking at Clola. "I can shoot as well as or better than anyone in the place! But Uncle Taran said he wants to find out if I'm safe before I can join a party on the moors."

Clola thought this was a wise precaution, but aloud she said:

"I am sure there are many other things you can do. What about fishing?"

She thought that Torquil's discontented expression lightened a little.

"I might do that," he muttered ungraciously.

"Can I come with you, please, Torquil? Can I come with you?" Jamie asked.

"I suppose so," he replied, "if Jeannie lets you."

"I'll soon run away from her!" Jamie said.

"My brothers have always envied you your salmon river," Clola said to Torquil.

For a moment she thought he was going to refuse to speak to her directly, but then he said:

"Hamish told me that."

"I am sure he did." Clola smiled. "I am glad that you and he are friends."

Clola wondered if Torquil's reply would be that he could never be friends with a Kilcraig. Then he said:

"He was decent to me when I was imprisoned in your Castle."

He said no more, but Clola thought that he had suddenly had an idea of how he should spend the day.

He ate the rest of his breakfast in silence while Jamie chattered away, and as he finished he said to one of the servants:

"Tell them to bring my pony to the front door. I'm going riding."

The servant went from the room and Jamie said:

"I thought you were going fishing and I could go with you."

"No. I have something else to do this morning," Torquil answered. "I might fish later this afternoon."

"I will tell you what I would like you to do, Jamie," Clola said. "Show me round the Castle."

The small boy seemed attracted by the idea, and

when breakfast was over they set out to explore every room and climbed up one of the turrets onto the roof.

The Castle was high, far higher than any other Castle Clola had ever seen, and from the battlements there was a most magnificent view over the whole countryside.

It was easy to realise how impregnable it had been in the past and how difficult it had been for the McNarns' enemies to attack this stronghold.

She was looking out towards the Loch and the mountains behind them, which she had seen last night from her bed-room, when Jamie said:

"You mustn't go near the edge. Jeannie says that some people when they look down get giddy and fall over."

"Jeannie is right," Clola said, "and it is very sensible of you to remind me. I hope you never come up here alone."

"I do sometimes," Jamie confessed, "but you mustn't tell Jeannie."

"I will not do that," Clola promised, "but please be very careful. I do not want to lose my first friend in the Castle."

"Is that what I am?" Jamie asked.

"My very first," Clola said, and she nearly added: "The only one!"

* * *

The Duke, Lord Hinchley, and Mr. Dunblane had an excellent day's sport.

It was early in the season and some of the birds were small, but they were all good enough shots to avoid killing the "Cheepers," as they were called.

As they walked home the Duke felt he had had one of the most satisfying shooting days he had ever enjoyed.

It was only as they neared the Castle that he began to wonder what had happened to Clola the night before.

He had in fact gone to her room, which he felt would be expected of him as a bridegroom, but he had not been as reluctant as he had anticipated or afraid of what he would find.

Watching Clola at dinner, he had been astounded by her beauty and even more by her elegance.

He was far too experienced where women were concerned not to realise that her gown would have graced Buckingham Palace.

In fact, with her dark hair, in which there were blue lights, her white skin, and her strange, mysterious eyes, he knew that his friends and certainly the Monarch would acclaim her a beauty.

He remembered his fears of becoming a laughing-stock and his decision never to allow his wife to go South. These were two of the things which no longer perturbed him.

At the same time, he could not dismiss so lightly his resentment at being forced into a marriage he did not want, nor could he overcome his dislike of the Kilcraigs as a Clan.

He was intelligent enough to realise that what was done could not be undone. For better or for worse, Clola was his wife, and the sooner they talked things over together and decided to make the best of a bad job, the better!

Lord Hinchley had said nothing about Clola in the presence of Mr. Dunblane, but the latter moved ahead of them as they neared the Castle.

He excused his haste on the plea that there were innumerable things for him to see to, among them the arrangements for Lord Hinchley's departure early in the morning, and the two friends walked alone.

"Shall I say what you know I am thinking?" Lord Hinchley asked.

The Duke did not pretend ignorance.

"She is certainly not what I feared and expected."

"She is beautiful!" Lord Hinchley said positively. "And she has, if I may so, the most haunting face I have ever seen."

"Haunting?" the Duke questioned.

"I find myself thinking," Lord Hinchley answered, "that a man would find it difficult to forget her."

The Duke made no comment, but he was listening as his friend went on:

"Perhaps it is her eyes. There is something about them which I cannot put into words. Perhaps it is the way they tip up a little at the corners, or the thickness of her eye-lashes."

He laughed as if at himself and added:

"I am quite certain, Taran, that in the olden days she would either have been burnt as a witch or worshipped as a goddess!"

"If you stay in the North much longer," the Duke said warningly, "you will develop a Celtic imagination, which is something Sassenachs are never supposed to have!"

Lord Hinchley laughed again, but as they entered the Castle he knew without being told that the Duke was in a very different frame of mind from what he had felt before his marriage.

As the Duke went upstairs he decided it would be polite to tell Clola that he was back before he went to his bed-room to bathe and change.

He looked into the Duchess's Room but to his surprise there was no-one there. He thought perhaps Clola was out in the garden or lying down, and went farther along the corridor.

It was then that he heard music, and it was not the music he had ever expected to hear in the Castle.

The Duke was a genuine music-lover.

It was fashionable in London to patronise the Opera. But for most of the *Beau Monde* it was an excuse for the ladies to be seen in their diamonds and for the gentlemen to "quiz" the Opera Dancers, from whose ranks their mistresses were usually chosen.

However, the King liked classical music and so did the Duke, and they both attended performances given by the Royal Philharmonic Society and gave concerts in their own homes, to which only their more musical friends were invited.

The Duke had been largely responsible for persuading the fine violinist Louis Spohr to accept the Philharmonic Society's invitation to visit England, and he considered him the equal of Mozart and Beethoven as a musician.

Now for a moment the Duke could not place the instrument he heard being played.

It had a clear, liquid, melodious sound and he knew the player was gifted, as whatever instrument it was vibrated in her hands.

He realised the sound came from the Red Drawing-Room, which was sometimes called the music room.

It was a room that had hardly ever been used in his father's time, but it contained an ancient harpsichord, a viola, and a harp.

The Duke smiled to himself. He had solved the question of what he was hearing.

It was the harp that stood in the Red Drawing-Room being played, and he could not remember ever before hearing it.

Quietly he opened the door.

Just as he had expected, Clola was sitting beside the huge golden harp and her long fingers were plucking from it a melody that the Duke recognised as having been composed by one of the great Masters.

She made a picture which his artistic instincts appreciated. Wearing a gown of yellow silk, her head silhouetted against one of the windows, she seemed to be enveloped in a light from the Heavens themselves.

Her small chin was lifted and her eyes looked ahead, and the Duke thought she was seeing sights that were not visible to him, as the curve of her lips showed that she was happy in a fantasy-world of her own.

Then, as he told himself he was being imaginative, Clola turned her head and saw him standing there.

As if he had taken her by surprise, her fingers faltered and then fell in silence.

The Duke walked across the room towards her.

"I had no idea you were a musician," he said. "I do not recall ever hearing that harp played before."

"It wanted tuning," she said, "and one or two of its strings need . . . replacing, but it is a very . . . fine one."

She spoke shyly, in a way which told the Duke she was nervous in his presence.

"We must see if we can find you something more modern than these instruments," he said with a gesture towards the harpsichord.

"That would be . . . delightful."

She looked up at him, then glanced away, her long, curved eye-lashes hiding her eyes.

"What were you playing? he asked.

She hesitated a second or so before she replied:

"It was . . . something I . . . composed myself . . . but I admit it was . . . inspired by Mozart."

"Can you play a pianoforte?"

"Yes."

"Then we had better buy one of the new ones made by John Broadwood."

Clola clasped her hands together and he saw the light in her eyes.

He did not know how much she had missed at Kilcraig Castle the pianoforte she had played at her grandmother's house in Edinburgh.

They were both silent and somehow words were not necessary.

Then as if she was compelled to break some strange spell which had renedered them speechless, Clola asked:

"Did you have a good shoot?"

"Very good!" the Duke replied in an absentminded way, as if his thoughts were elsewhere.

"I am . . . glad."

"I hope you have not found it lonely today?"

"Jamie was kind enough to show me round the Castle. I found it very . . . interesting."

It suddenly struck the Duke that it was something he would have liked to do himself. Then he thought that perhaps Jamie knew more about it than he did.

"I hope you were impressed," he said lightly.

"How could I . . . fail to . . . be?" Clola answered. "It is so . . . magnificent, and larger than I . . . expected."

"My grandfather, as you must realise, was extremely extravagant," the Duke said.

"You should be grateful that he was. Now you have a . . . treasure-house in the Highlands of which anyone would be . . . proud."

"I am not certain that where I am concerned 'proud' is the right word," the Duke said. "I expect you know I ran away to forget not only the Castle and everyone in it but also Scotland?"

He spoke as if he was being deliberately provocative. Clola looked at him with her strange eyes and said quietly:

"I have thought of how you must have . . . suffered. That is why Torquil and Jamie must . . . never feel the . . . same."

There was a note in her voice which told the Duke

that she really cared about his nephews, and it surprised him.

"I can see you are always ready to champion the underdog," he said with a smile.

They exchanged a few more words before the Duke went to his own room and Clola went to hers.

As she changed for dinner she found herself thinking so intently about the tall, handsome man who was her husband that she was able to ignore the baleful looks given her by Mrs. Forse.

They were sitting at the dining-table when there was the first sound of thunder in the distance and a sudden gust of wind came through the open windows to stir the curtains.

"I thought that would happen," Mr. Dunblane remarked.

"A thunder-storm?" the Duke enquired.

"It was far too hot today for the weather not to break," Mr. Dunblane replied.

"It was certainly hot," Lord Hinchley interjected. "I do not think I have ever before felt such intense heat when I was shooting."

"It will be cool enough in a short while," Mr. Dunblane said, and signalled to one of the servants to close the windows.

"I suppose it is going to rain," Lord Hinchley remarked. "A good thing this did not happen last night!"

Clola was thinking the same thing.

She knew that when there was a thunder-storm over the mountains it would gradually move to cover the whole countryside and after the thunder and lightning there would come torrential rain which would put the burns in spate and swell the rivers.

She hoped that all her Clansmen were home by now and she wondered too if Torquil was back in the Castle.

She had not seen him since breakfast-time and she

was not surprised, as he had said he was going riding, that he did not appear for luncheon.

Last night he had not been at dinner and she supposed the Duke had thought him still too young to dine with the grown-ups.

Her brothers when they were past fifteen always dined with their father, and she thought it was a mistake that Torquil was not being treated as an adult.

As soon as she had any say in what took place in what was now her home, she decided, this was one of the things she would change.

It was hard to think thtat this enormous, magnificent building was "home," but because she was practical in many ways Clola was determined to assume her rightful responsibility as soon as everyone became used to her presence.

She was well aware that a "new broom that sweeps clean" was never popular.

"I must not make suggestions, or alterations, until they have accepted me," she told herself.

She was sure that where Mrs. Forse was concerned that would never happen, and she had yet to find out how many other servants there were who would feel the same.

The Duke and Lord Hinchley were telling Mr. Dunblane of the large shoots they had attended in the South, the number of partridges and pheasants they had bagged, and obviously they did not expect her to join in the conversation.

She therefore watched the Duke as he sat at the head of the table, looking, she thought, more handsome than any man she had ever met before.

His air of authority and importance was, she was sure, exactly what a Chieftain should have, and doubtless it impressed not only his followers but also the Kilcraigs.

She would like to have an opportunity, she thought,

to talk to him alone, and she hoped that that would be possible tomorrow when Lord Hinchley had left, or perhaps later tonight. . . .

At the thought of that there was a faint flush on her cheeks, and the Duke, looking at her suddenly, wondered what it was that was making her look shy.

At the same time, as Lord Hinchley noticed, there was a mysterious expression in her eyes.

When dinner was over and the pipes had been played round the table, they retired to the Library because Mr. Dunblane had mentioned that there were some sporting prints in one of the books there which would interest the Duke and Lord Hinchley.

Clola took the opportunity of looking round and found a number of books she wished to read.

Then because she knew it would be expected of her to make the first move, she said good-night.

"I shall doubtless leave before you are up in the morning," Lord Hinchley said. "I have to hurry to reach Edinburgh before His Majesty arrives on the fourteenth, and may I say how much I shall be looking forward to meeting you again."

"Thank you," Clola said.

Lord Hinchley did not release her hand but went on:

"I want too to wish you and Taran every happiness together. You know he is my closest friend, and I am delighted that he should have such a beautiful wife."

"Thank . . . you," Clola said with a smile.

Lord Hinchley kissed her hand as she curtseyed.

As she rose she looked a little uncertainly at the Duke, wondering if he too would kiss her hand.

Then, realising that he had not said good-night, she thought it was intentional. She felt the blood rise in her cheeks, and, withdrawing, she hurried to her own room only to find, as she had feared, that Mrs. Forse was there waiting for her.

Tonight, because she was determined not to be upset again, Clola did not speak but allowed the woman to undress her in silence.

Only when she was nearly ready for bed did she say:

"That will be all, thank you, Mrs. Forse!"

Without speaking the woman left the room and Clola gave a little sigh of relief.

It was then that a violent clap of thunder made the windows rattle, and she thought again of the Clansmen, knowing that some at any rate would be drenched to the skin and might have to spend the night in the open.

The clap of thunder was followed by another and yet another.

Now the thunderstorm that had been drawing nearer all the evening appeared to be directly overhead and Clola thought that if the curtains were drawn the lightning would be like streaks of fire.

She got into bed, leaving two candles burning beside her, and she had hardly done so when the door opened.

She turned her head, expecting, though it seemed too soon, that it would be the Duke, but instead Jamie stood there, looking very small and lost in his long flannel nightgown.

"I'm alone," he said forlornly.

Clola knew only too well from the sound of his voice that he was frightened, and because she had brothers she said quickly:

"I am so glad you have come to see me. It is a horrible thunder-storm! I would like you to keep me company."

Jamie came into the room and shut the door behind him.

"Would you really?" he asked tremulously.

"Yes, I would," Clola answered.

As she spoke there was another explosion overhead.

With a movement like a small scared animal Jamie clambered onto her bed and slipped in beside her.

She put her arms round him and found that he was trembling.

"Are you—frightened?" he asked in a whisper.

"Not now that you are with me," Clola answered.

"Jeannie says the—giants on the mountains are—angry," Jamie said with a quiver in his voice.

"It is not giants who make the thunder-storms," Clola replied.

"No?"

"It is the naughty angels in the sky who push the clouds round until they run into each other! That's what makes the noise. It is only a game, but you know that if we bang two stones together we can see sparks, and when the clouds do it they make lightning."

"That must be rather fun!"

"I would rather like to push clouds round too," Clola said with a smile.

The idea excited Jamie's imagination and they talked about it for a little while until the small boy's voice became slower and slower and she knew he was falling asleep.

He was very soft and warm and smelt of soap and the lavender in which his nightshirts had obviously been kept.

The thunder moved farther away but Clola could hear the rain pouring down in torrents, as she had expected.

She was listening to it, thinking there was music even in its violence, when the communicating-door between her bed-room and the Duke's opened and he came in.

He had undressed and was wearing a long green velvet robe which nearly touched the floor, and the white frill of his nightshirt showed against his throat.

He did not speak but walked quietly towards her. Only when he reached the bed did he see that she was not alone.

He stood there, staring at her, seeing in the light from the candles her long dark hair falling over her shoulders, and her arms round Jamie with his red head against her breast.

She looked up at him and after a moment said very softly in a whisper:

"He was . . . frightened."

The Duke's eyes were on her face. For a moment he did not answer, then he said with a twist of his lips as if he was amused:

"I suppose it would be a mistake to wake him?"

"He is very young. I am . . . honoured that he should . . . come to me."

"Then—good-night."

He was still speaking in a whisper so that they should not disturb the sleeping child.

"Good-night," Clola answered.

The Duke lingered for a moment and Clola had the feeling that he was looking for something in her eyes, but she was not certain what it was.

Then abruptly he turned and went back to the door through which he had entered, and she thought that her heart beneath the heaviness of Jamie's head was beating in a strange manner.

* * *

It must have been two hours later when Clola awoke to hear a knock on the door.

In his sleep Jamie had moved away from her, turning over to sleep on the other side of the bed, with his back towards her.

She herself had not fallen asleep at once but had lain awake thinking about the Duke and wondering what they would have said to each other, or what might have happened, if the little boy had not been with her.

She felt that he was not hating her as he had done before.

At the same time, there were still barriers between them, barriers she could sense rather than to which she could put a name.

Now as she was startled to wakefulness she thought she had dreamt the knock at the door, until it came again.

She rose quickly from the bed, and picking up a wrap which lay over one of the chairs she put it on, slipping her feet as she did so into a pair of soft slippers.

As she opened the door she saw that an old man stood there with a lantern and she guessed he was the night-watchman.

"I'm real sorry te disturb Yer Grace," he said, "but there's a young gent'man at th' door an askin' for ye."

"A gentleman?" Clola repeated in surprise.

"He says he's yer brother, Yer Grace."

Clola was astonished and she said:

"I will come with you and speak to him."

She went out into the passage and shut the door behind her and they walked side by side towards the stairs, the light from the lantern guiding their steps.

"I didn'a know what te do, Yer Grace, when he comes an askin' for ye," the night-watchman said, "but most insistent he was he should speak te ye."

"You were quite right to wake me," Clola assured him. "It must be something very urgent!"

As she spoke, her thoughts were busy over what could have occurred. Had there been an accident involving her father on his way home?

It must, she thought, be something desperate for them to send for her in the middle of the night.

Then as she reached the top of the stairs, by the light of the candles in the sconces she could see her brother Hamish standing in the Hall below.

She hurried down to him, saying as she reached him:

"Hamish . . . what has happened? Why have you come here?"

"I have to speak to you. I have to tell you something," Hamish replied.

She thought he looked wild, his kilt covered in mud, his bare legs stained and very dirty.

She drew him to one side, out of earshot of the night-watchman, who tactfully removed himself to the outer Hall.

"What is it?" she asked.

"It's Torquil," Hamish answered. "The MacAuads have taken him prisoner!"

Clola stared at him in horror.

"What do you mean? What are you telling me?"

"We planned together that we should have a go at them just to teach them a lesson," Hamish said. "But while we were driving a calf over at the border, two men appeared from nowhere and caught hold of Torquil."

"Oh, Hamish, how could you do anything so stupid, so wrong, at this particular moment!" Clola cried.

"We planned it when Torquil was in prison," Hamish said, "and it seemed quite safe."

"Where is Torquil now?"

"That's what I came to tell you. I ran away before the men could catch me, but I watched them, hidden in the heather, and they've put Torquil in the watch-tower and have gone to get help."

"The watch-tower!" Clola exclaimed.

"They dragged him up the cliff and I expect locked him in. I have never been there so I didn't try to reach him. I thought it'd be best to get help."

He paused to say tentatively:

"Perhaps we could rescue him—before they come back."

Clola thought quickly.

"I will help you," she said, "but no-one must know about this. It would be terrible if the Duke learnt that Torquil had disobeyed him."

"How can you help?" Hamish asked.

"I will tell you when we get there," Clola said. "Go to the stables . . . no, wait a minute . . . I will give the order."

She went to find the night-watchman.

"My brother has brought me some bad news," she said to the old man. "A great friend is very ill. Will you please order two ponies for us? We will come to the stables, for I do not wish to disturb anyone."

The night-watchman looked surprised, but he was obviously used to obeying orders.

"I'll go te th' stables, Yer Grace, right awa'," he said.

"You go with him, Hamish," Clola said. "I will join you as soon as I have put on some clothes."

Then to her brother she said in a low voice so that only he could hear:

"Stick to my story about illness. Take care not to mention to anybody what has really occurred."

"No, of course not," Hamish said, indignant that she should think him so stupid.

Almost before she had finished speaking Clola was running up the stairs to her bed-room.

She pulled open the wardrobe, searched for a plain dress which had luckily been included among her many elaborate gowns, slipped it on with the warm jacket that went with it, and then tied a scarf over her head.

She put on the short boots she wore for walking on

the moors, which she found in the bottom of her wardrobe.

It took her only a few minutes to dress, and while she did so Jamie never moved but slept peacefully in the big bed.

Clola left the candles burning just in case he should wake and feel frightened; then, picking up a pair of leather gloves, she ran down the stairs and out through the front door, going towards the stables.

By the time she reached them a sleepy groom had been roused by the night-watchman and had saddled two ponies.

Hamish was already in the saddle, and as they started to move away from the Castle, Clola said to her brother:

"You have your skean dhu with you?"

"One in each stocking," Hamish answered.

Another time Clola would have laughed at the idea of wearing two of the short Scottish knives at the same time, but she knew the reason he wore two was to equip him for cutting loose an animal they were going to steal.

They moved with all possible speed over the moors towards the border. Clola in fact knew the Look-out well because it had always been one of the deep bones of contention between her Clan and the Mac-Auads.

Originally a Pictish Fort, the stones had been utilised by the MacAuads for building what they called a Look-out on a rocky cliff overlooking both the Kilcraig and the McNarn country.

As it was on the border of MacAuad land, Clola felt that it had been put there more as an act of defiance than for any serious use.

But it had in fact infuriated her brothers that the MacAuads if they wished could climb into their Look-out, which stood about twenty feet high, and stare over

Kilcraig land, while they were in the unfortunate position of not being able to overlook the MacAuads' land.

Clola must have been eleven when her second brother, Malcolm, had taken her with him to explore the Look-out, and, greatly daring, they had climbed the cliff.

It had been easier than Clola had expected and when they reached the top they had found their way into the Look-out itself.

It had a heavy studded oak door and Clola now remembered that there had been no lock. It was fastened by twine, which Malcolm had cut with his skean dhu, and they had gone inside to find a dark and smelly hole with only a wooden ladder up which those who wished to reach the top could climb.

Malcolm had been disgusted.

"I thought it was something better than this!"

"It looks more impressive outside then in," Clola had agreed.

"The MacAuads can keep it!" Malcolm said in disgust. "But we must leave them something to show we have been here."

They had nailed a rather dirty handkerchief to the door and tied Clola's hair-ribbon to the wooden steps inside.

It was not a very effective gesture but it had given Malcolm pleasure to think that he had braved and defied the MacAuads. But they had been far too frightened to tell Andrew what they had done, and certainly not their father.

Clola was thinking now that it was very unlikely that a lock had been added to the Look-out since she had last been there.

If she knew anything about the MacAuads it was that they were far too slap-dash to bother to exert themselves, unless it meant money in their pockets.

The rain had ceased, but the drive when the ponies

trotted down it was swimming with water and the heather was very wet.

Now the storm had almost died away in the distance and there was only an occasional rumble far in the East.

The moon, which had been full the night before, came out from between the clouds.

Clola and Hamish might have been able to find the Look-out without its assistance, but it was certainly easier when the light showed them the sheep-tracks running between the thick heather.

They were also able to avoid the gullies and, most important of all, the swollen burns.

Nevertheless, they had to cross one or two, and the ponies, being used to them, splashed through without difficulty where a horse from Edinburgh and certainly one from the South might have been afraid.

At last after they had been riding for a little over half-an-hour the Look-out came in sight.

"Did Torquil spend the day with you?" Clola asked.

"We met this morning," Hamish answered, "as we had arranged to do, and caught a salmon at the top of the river."

Clola had thought that perhaps that was what they were doing.

"What did you do with your ponies?"

"When we arrived here we tied them up over there," Hamish replied, pointing with his finger. "I was afraid to ride away in case the MacAuads heard me. I crawled through the heather, then ran all the way to the Castle."

Clola thought it was not surprising that he looked so dirty. But now it was dangerous to talk any more and she rode ahead, taking her pony as near to the bottom of the cliff as she dared.

Then she dismounted and Hamish did the same.

The ponies they had been given from the stables

were tough, strong, and used to long journeys over the moors without suffering from any fatigue.

The moment they were free they put their heads down, seeking the grass between the heather, and Clola was certain that they would not wander away.

"Follow me," she whispered to Hamish, and they went to the base of the cliff and looked up.

It was actually a rough gorge which started high up the hillside, going deeper on the MacAuad side until it ended at the Look-out.

There was quite a lot of water in the bottom of it, but Clola and Hamish splashed across regardless of wet feet and started to climb.

Frantically Clola tried to remember how she and Malcolm had managed all those years ago.

Fortunately, the moonlight was full on the cliff, so they could avoid the great bare rocks on which their feet slipped and keep to what footholds there were between them.

Clola found it hard to hold on because the rocks were wet, but somehow she managed to keep going, and she knew that gradually as they kept moving higher and higher she was nearly at the top.

As she pulled herself over the edge she was breathless and at the same time was listening intently just in case Hamish had been mistaken and one of the MacAuads had remained behind as a guard.

Nothing could be a worse disaster, she knew, than that not only Torquil but she too should become a prisoner of the MacAuads.

Then she saw the Look-out towering above her and there was no-one there, no sight or sound of the MacAuads.

She got to her feet and Hamish joined her.

They went to the door, which, as Clola had expected, was tied with thick twine, and there was no lock.

Without being told, Hamish drew his skean dhu from his stocking, cut the twine, and pulled the door open.

For a moment it was difficult to see what was inside because they themselves blocked the moonlight.

Then Clola realised that Torquil was lying on the floor, bound by a rope which tied his hands at his back, and that his mouth was covered with a piece of cloth, which gagged him.

First she pulled the gag from his mouth.

Then she took Hamish's other skean dhu and they hacked away. They got him free in a few minutes, and shaking the rope from his legs Torquil stood up.

Still without speaking, they slithered down the cliff and splashed across the burn to run towards the ponies.

Only as they reached them did Torquil say:

"We must collect the ponies Hamish and I rode here."

"Yes, of course," Clola agreed. "Ride behind Hamish—and we must hurry!"

The other ponies were only about a hundred yards away and as soon as they reached them Clola said:

"Hamish, go home! Get on your own pony and go at once. Torquil, you will have to lead the other one."

"I expect he'll follow us anyway," Torquil answered, but he took hold of the bridle, which meant, however, that they could not move so quickly.

Hamish left them, and Clola, looking back as she and Torquil rode ahead, asked:

"How could you do anything so crazy after what your uncle said to you?"

"I had promised Hamish. I couldn't go back on my word," Torquil said.

It was the perfect answer! Clola knew that for any Scot to break his word was bad enough, but for a McNarn to break it to a Kilcraig would be unthinkable!

They rode on. Then Torquil asked anxiously:

"Does Uncle Taran know you came to save me?"

"No, of course not," Clola replied. "No-one knows and no-one must ever know. Do you understand?"

She thought for a moment, then added:

"We will have to persuade the night-watchman and the groom not to talk. I think his name is Hector."

"He'll not talk," Torquil said.

"You must make sure of it," Clola said earnestly. "You know as well as I do what your uncle threatened if you got into mischief."

Torquil was silent. Then he said:

"It was jolly sporting of you to save me. How did you know how to reach the Look-out?"

Clola thought perhaps it was a mistake to say that she had been there with her brother Malcolm.

"We were lucky," she said. "Hamish had the sense to come and tell me what happened, and there was almost a full moon."

"We just had bad luck in being seen."

"It was not bad luck but crass stupidity to go at all!" Clola said crossly. "You have to promise me, Torquil, promise me on your word of honour, that you will never do such a thing again."

He did not answer and she pulled up her pony.

"Promise me," she said sharply, "or I might betray you to your uncle!"

"I promise!"

Torquil's tone was surly for a moment, then he changed it.

"I'm grateful to you too. Those MacAuads are rough and spiteful. They even hit me after tying me up."

Clola felt inclined to say: "It serves you right!"

But now they were getting nearer to the Castle and could ride side by side, and she could see that there was a mark on Torquil's cheek which she was certain would be a great purple bruise on the morrow. There was also a cut on his forehead.

She saw that his jacket-sleeve had been torn from the shoulder, presumably when fighting with the MacAuads, and his bare knees were bleeding from cuts and bruises.

She felt that he had had a lesson he would not forget.

Now they had reached the Castle drive and Clola thought with relief that it could not yet be four o'clock in the morning.

They could both go back to bed, she thought, and no-one would be any the wiser about the adventure in which they had taken part.

They reached the stables to find there was no-one about and the groom who had saddled their horses had obviously gone back to bed.

They put all three ponies into their stables, pulled off their bridles and saddles, and shut the doors quietly.

"I'll see you in the morning," Torquil whispered. "Shall we go in by the side door?"

"No, the night-watchman will be waiting for us at the front," Clola answered.

They hurried from the stables to the front of the Castle.

As Clola had expected, the door was unbolted. As they pushed it open the old man who had been waiting for them rose from a chair in the outer Hall, where he had been sitting with his lantern beside him.

"Ye're back, Yer Grace!" he exclaimed with an obvious note of relief in his voice.

"Yes, we are back," Clola answered, "and thank you for waiting for us."

She moved softly towards the stairs while Torquil hung back for a moment, and she knew he was telling the night-watchman to say nothing about the night's events.

Then as she started to climb the stairway he joined her.

"He'll be all right," he said.

She turned her head to smile at him and saw by the light of the candles how dishevelled he looked and thought she must look very much the same.

There was a turn on the staircase, the last six steps taking them onto the landing of the first floor, when Clola's heart gave a sudden leap.

Standing waiting for them, illuminated by the candles which had been lit since she left, was the Duke!

He was wearing the long green robe in which he had come to her bed-room and there was an expression on his face which made her and Torquil stop in their tracks.

He did not speak until Clola with Torquil just behind her had reached the last step of the stairs and was standing in front of him.

Then he asked:

"May I enquire where you have been at this time of the night?"

Clola heard Torquil draw in his breath, and quickly, having no time to think and therefore saying the first words that came into her mind, she replied:

"I had to . . . go and . . . meet someone . . . unexpectedly . . . and because I got into a little . . . trouble, Torquil came and . . . rescued me."

"Had to meet someone?" the Duke repeated. "And who might that be?"

"A . . . friend. Someone . . . who wished to . . . see me, and it was impossible to . . . wait until . . . morning."

"A friend!" the Duke exclaimed, and there was no mistaking the disbelief and contempt in his voice. "By 'friend' I presume you mean 'lover'!"

Clola gasped and as she did so it seemed as if the Duke grew taller, larger, and more overwhelming. Then he said in a voice which cut her like a knife:

"I knew that I was marrying a Kilcraig, but I did not realise she was also a harlot!"

His voice seemed to ring out. Then he turned and walked away, disappearing into the shadows of the corridor.

Torquil took a step forward but Clola put out her hand and laid it on his arm.

"No," she said. "Not now . . . not at this . . . moment, when he is so . . . angry. Wait, we . . . will think of . . . something tomorrow."

But she thought almost despairingly that there would be nothing she could say then, no explanation she could make which the Duke would understand or forgive.

Chapter Six

Clola awoke and realised it was late in the day.

Jamie must have slipped out without waking her and she knew that she had in fact been utterly exhausted when finally she fell asleep.

It had taken a long time because she had been deeply perturbed by the manner in which the Duke had spoken to her, and she had got back into bed feeling a despair that was worse than anything she had ever known before.

For a long time she had turned over and over in her mind what explanation she could give him other than the one that had come spontaneously to her lips when she had found him standing at the top of the stairs.

It seemed to her that there was no way in which she could excuse herself without involving Torquil.

Though she felt it was extremely reprehensible of him, after all that had been said, to go with Hamish into the MacAuad country, she was aware that it would have been almost impossible for him to admit to a Kilcraig that he was afraid of the consequences.

She thought despairingly that the Duke would never

understand because he had lived too long in the South, where men would break their word far more easily and lightly than a Scot would ever do.

"What can I do? What can I do?" she asked herself over and over again.

Although mentally she was in a high state of tension, eventually, because climbing the cliff had been physically fatiguing, she fell asleep.

On waking she realised that she was stiff and she thought too she might have caught a cold.

But nothing was of any importance except to try by some means, though she had no idea how, to make the Duke believe that she had not, as he had inferred, been meeting a lover.

She turned a dozen different explanations over in her mind, only to find that they all sounded unconvincing and untruthful.

She rang the bell and after some delay Mrs. Forse came into the room to say in her hostile voice:

"Ye were asleep, an' I left ye."

"I was tired," Clola said simply. "But now I must get up."

Mrs. Forse had crossed the room and was pulling back the curtains.

"There's nae hurry for Yer Grace," she said. "The gentlemen have all gone awa' and there's only the children and yerself left in the Castle."

"The gentlemen have left?" Clola questioned.

"Aye. His Grace and His Lordship were awa' firrst thing."

"And Mr. Dunblane?" Clola asked.

She thought that it was Mr. Dunblane to whom she must turn in her difficulties.

It was he who had persuaded the Duke to send Torquil to school and to Oxford; and she was certain that if she confided in him he would be sympathetic and understanding.

"Mr. Dunblane has also gone te Edinburgh," Mrs. Forse said.

There was something almost triumphant in her tone, as if she was glad that Clola was left behind.

Clola got out of bed, wincing as she did so because her knee was scratched and bruised from climbing the cliff.

She had also broken the nails on her fingers and she felt as if the pain of it all added to the unhappiness in her mind.

"Ye're stiff," Mrs. Forse said, as if it had suddenly struck her that Clola was moving more slowly than usual. "I'll awa' and fetch ye sommat te ease it."

"Please do not bother. I shall be all right," Clola replied. "I think perhaps I have caught a cold."

"It's nae trouble," Mrs. Forse said, and went from the room.

Because she felt so low, Clola was almost grateful that the woman who had been so hostile waas now being more amenable.

It was unreasonable, but she felt as if the Duke had deserted her by leaving for Edinburgh sooner than she had expected.

She had meant when she could talk to him to tell him how well she knew Edinburgh and all the people in it.

She had hoped when she explained how long she had lived there with her grandmother that he would suggest taking her with him to meet the King.

Now she thought she had been foolish in not explaining how she had only recently come North.

Yet there had been no opportunity at the table when the men were talking of sport, and the first night she was sure that the Duke had deliberately left her out of the conversation.

Last night had been the only time, and she had actually thought of telling him after dinner a little about her life.

But Lord Hinchley had been there and somehow it seemed egotistical to talk about herself at all intimately with a stranger present.

She had imagined that there would be plenty of time, but now it was too late and the Duke was gone.

Although she longed to join him she knew it would be impossible to travel alone and without Mr. Dunblane's assistance in making all the arrangements.

Clola was nearly dressed when Mrs. Forse returned. In her hands she carried a tray on which reposed a glass of warm milk.

"I've put some herrbs in it," the woman said. "It'll tak' awa' th' stiffness an' prevent a cold."

"It is very kind of you."

Actually Clola disliked warm milk but she had no wish to hurt Mrs. Forse's feelings by refusing the drink she had taken so much trouble to bring her.

She took a sip and found there was honey mixed with the milk and it therefore was not unpleasant.

"You are knowledgeable about herbs?" she asked. "My old Nurse used to know a great deal about them and as children we were always given herbs when we were ill."

"There's been a herrb-garden at th' Castle fer at least twa centuries," Mrs. Forse said, "and the people all come te me wi' their ailments."

"You must tell me sometime which herbs are efficacious," Clola said with a smile.

She finished the milk, thanked Mrs. Forse, and when her gown was buttoned she walked towards the Duchess's Room.

There was no-one about and she guessed that because it was already afternoon the boys would have had their luncheon and gone out into the sunshine.

It was a bright day after the storm last night and she thought she would like to walk down and see what undoubtedly would be a spate in the river.

When she appeared, the Butler came into the room to ask if she would like anything to eat.

"I have just had some milk, thank you," Clola said, "and I will wait until tea-time. I am sure you have cleared away everything by now."

"It'd be nae trouble to bring Your Grace something fresh," the Butler said. "I wouldn't like te see Your Grace hungry."

He seemed a kindly man, and Clola replied:

"Thank you, but I will wait until tea-time. I suppose Mr. Torquil and Master Jamie have gone out?"

"That's right, Your Grace."

Clola walked to the Music Room.

Whenever she felt perturbed, worried, or unhappy, it was always music that could bring her solace, and she would forget everything else when she played.

She remembered how the Duke had promised her a pianoforte, but she thought now that he would bring her back nothing but a renewal of his hatred for her and the rest of the Kilcraigs.

Because the thought was so depressing she felt the tears prick her eyes; then, fighting her emotions, she sat down at the harp and started to play.

A composition by Mozart came to her mind and her fingers, but after she had played for only a few minutes she suddenly felt very tired.

She was in fact so sleepy that she left the harp to sit down on the sofa. . . .

The next thing she knew was that the Butler and the footman were bringing in the tea-things and she must have been asleep for nearly two hours.

Her head felt heavy and it was hard to open her eyes to see that they had brought her all sorts of delicious scones, griddle cakes, and shortbread. But while she found it hard to eat more than a mouthful, she drank the fragrant tea thirstily.

After she had finished, Clola sat on the sofa feeling it too much of an effort to move or even to think.

She had meant to ask Torquil if he would like to dine with her, but when she went along to her own room to change for dinner Mrs. Forse said:

"Ye're looking real played oot, Yer Grace. Why do ye no get inta bed, and I'll bring ye yer dinner?"

"I am sure I must be getting a cold," Clola said, "and I do feel very tired."

"Then just ye do as I suggest, Yer Grace, and I'll fetch ye another drink o' my herrbs, and that'll soon put ye on yer feet again."

Clola leant back against her pillows, with her eyes closed, thinking it was strange that she should feel so exhausted.

It must be due, she thought, to the softness of her life in Edinburgh.

She remembered how before leaving home she could have walked all day on the moors and then stayed up half the night without it having any more effect on her than it had on her brothers.

Mrs. Forse brought her the same honey-sweetened milk and she drank it quickly, ready to take anything which would make her feel better.

"Yer dinner'll be a-coming in a wee while," Mrs. Forse said.

If it came Clola was not aware of it, for she had fallen asleep while planning that as soon as she was well enough she would ride over to Kilcraig Castle to see her family.

The following morning she felt worse, and because she told herself it was sensible to eat she forced herself to consume some of the breakfast which Mrs.

Forse brought to her, but was persuaded to stay in bed.

Luncheon came and with it another glass of milk. Clola drank only a little of it, feeling that it was too sweet to take at the same time as the Chef's delicious food.

She felt stronger in the afternoon and decided that her illness was passing and tomorrow she would be up again.

"Ye didn'a drink yer milk at luncheon, Yer Grace," Mrs. Forse complained.

"I know, but there were so many other nice things," Clola said in a conciliatory tone, feeling that the woman had taken a lot of trouble.

"Tonicht, I've ordered some special soup te put strength intae ye," Mrs. Forse said, "an' there's chicken with cream sauce which th' chef'll be disappointed if ye dinna eat."

"I will do my best," Clola promised. "It is ridiculous to feel so weak and lie about when there are so many things I want to do."

Because she had felt better after luncheon, when her dinner came she made a great effort to eat a little of every dish.

The soup was certainly delicious and so was the chicken with a thick sauce poured over it.

There were other dishes from which she could choose but she sent them away, thinking she had had enough.

An hour later Mrs. Forse came in with what she called her "herbal night-cap."

"I've made it from herrbs which I plucked only this morning, Yer Grace," she said. "Fresh and sweet they are, they'd put heart intae a dying man!"

"Thank you, but I will drink it later," Clola said.

"Drink it the noo, while it's just th' right temperature," Mrs. Forse insisted. "I must get Yer Grace well—otherwise, what'll His Grace have te say when he returrns?"

Clola thought that she would certainly need her strength to face the Duke again.

Because she felt too weak to argue with Mrs. Forse she drank the herbal drink, finding it a trifle unpleasant, but she was too polite to say so.

She went to sleep, then awoke in the darkness to find herself gripped with almost intolerable pains in the stomach.

It was so excruciating that after enduring it for some minutes she rang the bell because she was frightened at the violence of it.

Mrs. Forse came hurrying into the room.

"Ye rang, Yer Grace?"

"Yes, Mrs. Forse. I am in pain. Terrible pain. I cannot think what it is."

"It's going too long wi'oot proper food, Yer Grace, an' a chill in the stomach often results in th' cramps."

"Yes, of course, that must be it," Clola agreed. "I must see a Doctor in the morning, but is there something you can give me in the meantime to make it more endurable?"

"That's what I thought ye'd ask," Mrs. Forse said, "an' I've brought sommat with me."

She gave Clola a milky white liquid in a small glass.

She drank it off and almost immediately the pain ceased, but once again she felt intolerably sleepy and knew nothing more. . . .

* * *

Clola awoke, heard a clock chime and realised it was midnight.

She remembered it had been the early hours of the morning when she had rung for Mrs. Forse.

A sudden thought struck her, so extraordinary that she could hardly credit it, and yet what other explanation was there?

She had missed a whole day!

With an effort she forced her brain to think back, remembering the pain that had gripped her, the milky drink that Mrs. Forse had brought with her and which had sent her to sleep.

Why had Mrs. Forse brought the drink into the room with her?

It was strange, very strange, Clola thought, and now suddenly, unaccountably, something else came back to her.

She had been aroused from sleep to drink again, but why was it so indistinct, just the memory of something trickling down her throat, not once but twice. Perhaps more.

She thought she was in a nightmare and perhaps had a fever and she would raise her hand to her forehead.

But when she tried to do so it was impossible. Her hands seemed to be made of lead and she could not move them from her sides.

The shock of it seemed to make her think a little more clearly: now she knew what was happening and was possessed by the terror of the knowledge.

Then she became aware that someone was near her, someone she had known before, calming her, protecting her—it was the Grey Lady!

She was so real that Clola spoke to her in her mind even though it was impossible for her lips to move.

"What has happened to . . . me? Why am I . . . like . . . this?"

The Grey Lady gave her the answer:

"You are being poisoned!"

Clola gave a little cry.

Poisoned by Mrs. Forse . . . and she was helpless . . . unable to move.

She desperately wanted to close her eyes and go to sleep again, but with a superhuman effort she made herself think back.

Now she was certain that not one day but perhaps several had passed while she was unconscious.

"Help me! Help me!" she cried to the Grey Lady.

It was as if she drew nearer and Clola could feel her hand on her forehead, soothing and calming her.

"What can I . . . do? I do not . . . want to die!"

It was a cry in her heart, and yet still her lips did not move. She felt her whole body was numb and . . . paralysed.

"Help will come!"

She could hear the words spoken.

"Help will . . . come?" she asked. "But how . . . and from . . . where?"

"You must be brave, you must fight."

Again the words were in her mind, just as if they had been spoken aloud.

Clola tried to raise her hand and again found it impossible, but it seemed as if the very effort made her breathe more easily.

'That is what I must do,' she thought to herself, 'breathe deeply. Try to clear my mind so that I can think.'

She breathed and went on breathing steadily in the darkness, until she saw the first streak of light at the sides of the curtains.

It was another day, perhaps a day which would bring her death, the death she could not avoid.

"Help me! Help me!" she cried again to the Grey Lady, and thought that the Lady had gone and she was alone.

For a moment sheer panic swept over Clola, but she told herself she had to fight and being afraid would not help.

She went on breathing deeply and watching the light creeping in between the curtains.

It suddenly struck her that it was coming from only one window instead of three; then, as it grew brighter, the outline of the four-poster bed in which she had slept in the Duchess's Room was not there.

Incredulously, as more light came in from the only window, Clola found that she was in a room she had never seen before.

It was small, so very much smaller than the room in which she had slept when she came to the Castle.

Then she realised that the room was round and she knew where she was—in one of the turrets!

For a moment it seemed so incredible that she thought she must be mad or, as she had thought at first, delirious.

Then she was aware of the furniture.

It was plain, sparse, and there was a small hearth in the curve of the wall and a second door which she knew would lead out onto the battlements.

How could she have been brought here without being aware of it—and for what reason?

It flashed through her mind that she was a prisoner as Torquil had been—but not the prisoner of the Duke, who was away.

No . . . a prisoner of Mrs. Forse!

Clola remembered the hatred in her eyes and the way she had spoken on her wedding-night.

She knew now that she should have asked Mr. Dunblane that very first evening if he would find another woman to act as her lady's-maid.

But it had seemed impossible to cause trouble the moment she arrived in the Castle.

Yet now she was in Mrs. Forse's power and it seemed unlikely that she would survive the poison that was being poured into her.

'I will take no more of the food and drink she brings,' Clola decided.

Then she knew that as she could not move her hands it would be impossible to prevent Mrs. Forse from pouring her pernicious herbs down her throat as she must have done when she was too drugged to know what was happening to her.

She would die!

Die by the hand of a woman who hated her because she was a Kilcraig, and there was no-one to rescue her from this turret where Mrs. Forse must have had her conveyed.

It was all so terrifying that Clola closed her eyes at the sheer horror of it, but, afraid that she might fall once again into a drugged sleep, she forced them open and went on breathing deeply, as she had before, trying to get more oxygen to her heart and to her brain.

As the light grew brighter and brighter she could now see everything in the room clearly and thought it was a condemned cell from which she could never escape!

She tried to move her hands again and this time succeeded in raising them an inch or so off the mattress.

But her legs still felt as if they did not belong to her, and it was impossible to sit up.

"Help me! Help me!" Clola cried to the Grey Lady, thinking that if only she could move she might open the door and somehow get downstairs to find someone to help her.

Then she heard a sound and stiffened.

It would be Mrs. Forse, she thought, coming with more of her evil herbs.

She wanted to scream but knew that even if she could do so it would be impossible for anyone to hear from the very top of the great Castle.

Then as she waited, so frightened that even her

breath seemed to have stopped, a door opened slowly and creakily, and it was the door onto the battlements.

A small face appeared round it and she saw that it was Jamie.

"Jamie!" Clola called his name but it was only a croak which came from her lips.

He opened the door a little farther and came into the room.

"Mrs. Forse said we weren't to come near you as you had a fever," he said, "but I came over the roofs to tell you I was sorry."

Clola forced herself to speak.

"Jamie!" she said in a croaking whisper. "Fetch . . . Torquil to . . . help me . . . fetch him . . . quickly!"

"You want Torquil?" Jamie asked. "You look ill—very ill!"

"I am ill . . . tell . . . Torquil to come . . . quickly . . . quickly . . . and do not . . . let anyone . . . hear you. . . ."

It was terribly hard to say the words, but she saw that Jamie understood.

As if he was frightened by her appearance and her croaking voice, he turned and ran back through the door onto the battlements, shutting it behind him.

Clola closed her eyes.

To speak, she thought, had been the greatest effort she had ever made in her life.

Her mind drifted away for a moment into the darkness and she was sinking, sinking lower and lower until she was aware of someone leaning over her.

She knew who it was before she opened her eyes to look, knew it by the unmistakable sense of evil.

Then she felt Mrs. Forse's arms go round her.

"Come along, Yer Grace," she said in a voice that was almost mesmeric. "Come for a walk, then ye'll nae longer feel ill."

She pulled Clola up into a sitting position.

"Leave . . . me . . . alone," Clola tried to say, but the words did not sound very coherent.

"I'm a-doing what's best for ye an' best for the McNarns," Mrs. Forse said.

She was speaking in a low voice as if she were talking partly to herself and partly to a child.

"Come along the noo, then ye'll know nothin' more —nothin' at all!"

By this time she had lifted Clola's legs onto the floor, and now putting her arm round her waist she pulled her onto her feet, except that they would not hold her.

She would have sagged and fallen if Mrs. Forse had not held her up.

"Let . . . me . . . go!" Clola managed to articulate.

"Noo, ye're a-goin' te die!" Mrs. Forse said. "Ye're going te die by th' hand o' a McNarn—an' there's justice in that!"

She suddenly chuckled in an evil way which made Clola relise through a haze of horror that she was insane.

She wanted to fight the woman and push her away, but she could not move her hands and Mrs. Forse was carrying her bodily across the small room to where Clola could see the open turret door.

"No! No!" she cried. "You cannot . . . do this!"

"Ye'll die!" Mrs. Forse ejaculated. "Ye'll die an' for th' vengeance o' ma ancestors I'll thank th' Lawd."

She paused a moment to push the heavy door a little farther open. Then she said:

"Ma son Euan'll avenge those who died by th' hand o' th' English when he shoots doon their King, who dares te set his blood-stained feet on th' soil o' Scotland".

As she spoke out, she dragged Clola onto the battlements.

There was a sharp wind and the coolness of it on

her face seemed to revive a little of Clola's strength.

She managed to put out her hands to hold on to the high point of a crenellated battlement.

"No!" she managed to cry. "No!"

"Look doon an' see how far ye'll fall," Mrs. Forse said. "Ye'll die when ye reach the ground, an' they'll say: 'Puir lady, she walked from her room in her fever, an' fell!' "

She laughed and it was a horrible sound.

"An' who'll mourn a Kilcraig?"

Clola could feel the rough stone of the battlement beneath her fingers, then Mrs. Forse started to pull her along to the lower part, where the wall only reached to her knees.

Her arms were strong and Clola knew despairingly that it was only a question of seconds before she would no longer be able to hold on but must fall as Mrs. Forse intended.

"Die!" Mrs. Forse cried, and her voice seemed to ring out. "Die, an' may th' Devil take yer black soul down inta Hell!"

She pulled with all her strength as she spoke and Clola felt herself about to fall.

She looked down, and the ground far away beneath her was swimming before her eyes. Then there was a sudden yell and the sound of heavy footsteps coming over the roof.

Mrs. Forse had almost pulled her free of the higher battlements to which she was clinging when Clola felt strong arms go round her to pull her back to safety.

"Let her die, Master Torquil!" Mrs. Forse screamed. "Her's a Kilcraig an' she has te die!"

"Let go of her, you wicked woman!" Torquil shouted.

He had one arm round Clola, but Mrs. Forse was still pulling at her and Torquil struck out.

He hardly touched Mrs. Forse but she stepped back

to avoid the blow and her feet slipped on the damp lead of the roof.

As she did so, she released her hold on Clola and overbalanced and fell through the opening in the crenellation where she had meant to push her victim.

She screamed and Clola saw her face contort, her eyes wide with terror and her mouth open, before she disappeared from view.

Clola gave a sob which was the only sound she could make as Torquil dragged her back through the door into the turret.

With his arms round her—for otherwise she would have fallen to the ground—he stood looking at the small bed and the partially furnished room.

"You can't stay here," he muttered.

Then as he realised that she was too weak to do anything for herself, he picked her up in his arms and carried her very carefully down the stairs.

He was tall and strong for his age and Clola was very light and weak from all she had been through.

It was not difficult for him to take her down the twisting turret staircase, then to descend the wider one which led from the top floor of the house down to the first, where the Duchess's bed-room was situated.

He was halfway down the second flight of stairs when Jamie came running from behind him.

"You've saved her! Oh, Torquil, you've saved her!" the little boy cried.

"Go and fetch Jeannie," Torquil said. "Tell her to come quickly."

It was the voice of command and Jamie ran past him to obey.

They had almost reached the Duchess's bed-room when Clola remembered.

Her brain felt as if it was packed with cotton-wool,

so that it was too great an effort to speak and she felt too weak to attempt it.

All she could see behind her closed eyes was Mrs. Forse's open mouth and wide-eyed terror.

Then she made herself remember what the woman had said.

"Tor-quil!" Clola forced the name between her lips.

"It's all right," Torquil replied. "You are safe. She's dead. She can't hurt you any more."

"Her . . . son!" Clola gasped. "Her son . . . Euan . . . means to . . . kill the . . . King!"

She felt Torquil's arms stiffen in astonishment and a moment later Clola felt him put her down on the bed.

She thought he might go away and tried to reach out her hand to prevent him.

"You . . . must . . . tell . . . the Duke," she murmured faintly. "Go . . . to Edinburgh . . . warn him!"

She knew that Torquil was staring at her as if he thought she had taken leave of her senses, and she said:

"Think of the . . . Clan. . . . For a . . . McNarn to . . . kill the King . . . it . . would be . . ."

There was no need to say any more.

"I understand," Torquil interrupted. "I'll go at once. I'll take two men with me and if it's possible we'll get there in time."

"Hurry . . . hurry!" Clola insisted.

She heard Torquil's feet running down the corridor, and she shut her eyes.

Vaguely, as she drifted into unconsciousness, she remembered the Grey Lady saying:

"Fate has sent you. There are things that only you can do!"

* * *

The Duke had travelled to Edinburgh in a black rage and there was nothing Lord Hinchley could say to disperse it.

Because of the delay caused by the Duke's wedding and Lord Hinchley's desire to shoot, they all travelled by sea, which was quicker.

Mr. Dunblane had chartered a ship which was large and comparatively comfortable, and the sea being calm, the voyage only took a day.

So Lord Hinchley was spared two days of jolting over bad roads which he would otherwise have been forced to endure.

The Duke found the whole of Edinburgh *en fête* and it seemed extraordinary that such elaborate preparations should have been made to welcome the King from England.

There was no doubt that the Scots for the moment had put aside their hatred and their resentment of the past, and the gaily decorated city and the obvious excitement in the air seemed to forecast a better relationship in the future.

The Duke found on arrival that His Majesty was to stay with the sixteen-year-old Earl of Dalkeith at Dalkeith Palace.

He was also informed that every house in Edinburgh was packed from floor to ceiling with the nobility who had poured in from every part of Scotland for this auspicious occasion.

He had however been for many years a friend of the Duke of Hamilton, and he knew that if it was possible the Duke would entertain him at Holyrood Palace.

The Duke of Hamilton was hereditary Keeper of the ancient Palace, which had been burnt by the soldiers of Cromwell.

It was however later repaired and enlarged, and the

Young Pretender, Prince Charles Stuart, had resided there for some time during the Rebellion of 1745.

The Duke knew that a great part of the building was now uninhabited, but the Duke of Hamilton had lodgings within it when he came to Edinburgh, as had several others of the Scottish nobility.

The Duke of Hamilton welcomed the Duke with open arms and assured him that there was plenty of room in his part of the building for both himself and Mr. Dunblane.

Lord Hinchley had arranged before he left England that he would stay at Dalkeith Palace with the King.

The first night the Duke arrived he was able to dine quietly with the Duke of Hamilton and a few friends, because although the *Royal George* had dropped anchor, His Majesty was not due to land at Leith until the following day.

The Duke of Hamilton discussed with the Duke the arrangements that had been made especially concerning the Cavalry Review on Portobello Sands.

Then as the port was passed round the table he said:

"There is a rumour, which may be entirely untrue, that you are married, Strathnarn."

The Duke's eyes darkened for a moment, but because there was nothing else he could say he replied:

"Yes, that is true."

"This is most unexpected," The Duke of Hamilton said, "but we must certainly congratulate you and give you all our good wishes. There is only one thing I cannot understand."

"What is that?" the Duke enquired.

"Why you have not brought your beautiful Duchess with you."

The Duke looked surprised but the Duke of Hamilton smiled.

"I have known Clola since she first came to Edinburgh when she was fifteen. She was lovely then, but I can assure you, Strathnarn, that last winter at least half the eligible bachelors of Scotland laid their hearts at her feet."

"That is true," another man interposed, "but she would have none of us. I always suspected that her grandmother was keeping her for someone as grand as Strathnarn."

The Duke was too astonished to make any reply, but, as he seemed reluctant to talk of his new wife, the Duke of Hamilton did not refer to her again.

When the party broke up, Lord Brora, who was an old friend and often stayed in London, accompanied the Duke to his rooms.

The moment they were alone Lord Brora said fiercely:

"When did you marry Clola, and why was I not told about it?"

"We were married only a few days ago," the Duke said coldly.

"It is intolerable! Absolutely intolerable that you should sweep her off in this manner!" Lord Brora exclaimed in a strange tone. "If I had any guts I would blow a piece of lead through you!"

"What the devil are you talking about?" the Duke enquired. "Do you know my wife?"

"Know her?" Lord Brora's voice was raw. "I have asked her to marry me a thousand times and the answer was always the same—no!"

He walked across the room, his kilt swinging from his hips as if it expressed the anger he was feeling.

"Have you not enough women in the South," he asked, "that you should come North to carry off the most desirable woman in all Scotland under our noses?"

"Are you telling me that Clola lived in Edinburgh?" the Duke asked.

"Of course, she has lived in Edinburgh for the last three years," Lord Brora replied. "She was brought up here by her grandmother, one of the most outstanding and certainly the most intelligent women North of the Tweed."

The Duke was silent and Lord Brora went on:

"Surely Clola must have told you that she was acclaimed, fêted and loved by everyone—especially by me?"

"She has certainly never mentioned you," the Duke said truthfully.

"It would be like her not to boast of her conquests," Lord Brora said, and his voice softened. "But I am asking myself, Strathnarn, how I can live without her."

There was a note in his voice which told the Duke that the man who had been his friend for some years was suffering. But he did not know what he could do about it.

"How did you persuade her into accepting you?" Lord Brora went on after a moment. Then he gave an exclamation. "I know what it is! You are both musical! How could I compete with that when I cannot tell one note from another?"

"Clola is musical?" the Duke asked tentatively.

"Of course she is musical. She plays like an angel and sings like one too. If she had not been a lady and wealthy she could have made a fortune as a professional!"

The Duke was stunned into silence.

Vaguely at the back of his mind he remembered assuming he was marrying someone uncivilised and uneducated.

"Well, I am going to bed!" Lord Brora said sharply.

This told the Duke that he felt too upset at what

had occurred to stay talking to him, but as he reached the door Lord Brora added:

"What I cannot understand is why you did not bring Clola with you."

He gave a short laugh.

"I suppose the answer is that you are too jealous to let any of her old friends near her."

He left the room and the Duke rose to stand at the diamond-paned window, looking out at the courtyard of the Palace.

He did not see the moonlight on the roofs and chimneys. Instead, he saw two mysterious eyes with flecks of gold in them and he heard a soft voice repeating the Oath of Allegiance.

The Duke did not sleep well that night, nor the next.

* * *

The King arrived and was delighted with his Reception and with the large number of the nobility who were in attendance upon him.

His own Suite consisted of many of the Duke's more personal friends.

Like Lord Brora, as soon as they heard that he was married they bombarded him with questions, many of which he found impossible to answer.

The King's eyes were twinkling when he congratulated him.

"Caught at last, eh, Taran?" he said. "And from all reports, the Duchess is so lovely and so attractive that I cannot understand why you are hiding her from me."

"She was unable, Sire, to come to Edinburgh so soon after our marriage."

It was the excuse that the Duke had given to all the other enquirers, but he could not help his voice from becoming more stiff and more reserved each time he had to repeat it.

"Bring her South, my boy," the King said. "Bring her to London as soon as possible. I am determined to make the acquaintance of this paragon of beauty and virtue, so do not try my curiosity too high!"

The Duke bowed his acceptance, remembering his decision to leave his wife, whom he had been forced into marrying, alone in Scotland.

His Majesty held a Levee at Holyrood Palace on August 17, at which the Duke was in attendance.

Besides the Chieftains of the Clans, many noblemen and gentlemen appeared in Highland dress, among whom, together with the Duke, were the Dukes of Hamilton and Argyll and the Earl of Breadalbane.

After the Levee, His Majesty held a Privy Council, and on Monday a Court and closed audience, also at Holyrood Palace.

The following day a Drawing-Room Reception was attended by all the most important ladies in Edinburgh, and there again the Duke was bombarded with questions as to why Clola was not with him.

"At least she will not eclipse us all as she did at the Balls last winter!" the Marchioness of Queensbury exclaimed.

While the Countess of Elgin added:

"But she was so sweet and unspoilt by her success that it was impossible to be jealous of her."

After this, there were processions, meetings, inspections, and a special Banquet given in Parliament House by the Lord Provost, so the Duke hardly had time to think.

Finally, everyone was looking forward to the Cavalry Review that was to take place on Portobello Sands.

The Duke was surprised to learn that fifty thousand spectators were expected and the whole Corps of Volunteer Troops numbered over three thousand.

He learnt that Mr. Dunblane had arranged for fifty of the McNarn Yeomanry, in which his father had taken a special interest, to represent the Clan.

Each Clan had its own Standard, Badge, and Piper, and when the Duke saw the McNarns rehearsing the day before the Review, he had been very impressed by their appearance.

They were just as smart as, if not smarter than, those under the command of the Earl of Breadalbane, who wore yellow plumes in their bonnets and crests on their right arms.

The Duke of Argyll was to lead the Celtic Society, a body of one hundred Highlanders, all superbly dressed, each in his own Clan tartan with a belted plaid.

Sir Euan McGregor, carrying the same broadsword which his grandfather had used at the Battle of Prestonpass, led the Clan Gregor. He wore an outstanding red tartan and each of the Clansmen had a branch of fir in his bonnet.

The Marchioness of Stafford had sent fifty Highlanders from Dunrobin, and Lady Gwydir had sent a gallant band of Drummonds, their Badge a holly bough.

There was a great deal of rivalry and a certain amount of jealousy amongst the Clansmen, but the Duke felt that the McNarns would hold their own and he found himself feeling extremely proud of their appearance.

Just before he left the parade Mr. Dunblane said to him:

"There are several men who would like a word with Your Grace, if you can spare the time."

"What about?" the Duke enquired.

"Their problems," Mr. Dunblane replied.

"Their problems?" the Duke queried.

There was a faint smile on Mr. Dunblane's face as he said:

"It is traditional, as you will appreciate, that they may bring their problems to their Chieftain as in ancient days. It is in fact a compliment."

"Do you really expect me to solve the problems of these men?" the Duke asked. "What do I know of their lives when I have lived in the South for so long?"

"They trust you, they believe in you, and they will do what you say," Mr. Dunblane said.

The Duke thought for a moment.

"Very well," he replied. "I will speak to them, but God knows if the advice I give them will be any good."

"I think you underestimate your sympathy with your own people," Mr. Dunblane said quietly.

Before the Duke could think of a reply, Mr. Dunblane went to fetch the men who wished to see him.

To his own surprise, the Duke found himself giving decisions on problems covering land, cattle, family difficulties, and even in one instance whether a man was too young to take a wife.

As he rode back to Holyrood Palace with Mr. Dunblane beside him he said:

"I suppose this is another way in which you are trying to trap me into assuming my responsibilities and staying in the North?"

"I am not trying to trap you," Mr. Dunblane replied. "It is perhaps your heart that will do that."

"I have no heart!" the Duke said harshly.

He thought as he spoke that he had put too much emphasis on the word.

They reached the Palace and rode in through the great gates. As they drew their horses to a standstill outside the door which led to the private apartments, the Duke saw a young figure come racing towards him and stared in disbelief.

"Torquil!" he exclaimed.

Then his nephew was at his side, his words tumbling over themselves in his anxiety to make the Duke understand the urgency of what he had come to tell him.

Chapter Seven

"Now try an' rest, Your Grace, and, if ye can, have a quiet nap," Jeannie admonished. "I'm taking Master Jamie away to th' river and we won't be back 'til it's nearly his bed-time."

Jeannie spoke in the kind but firm way that Clola remembered her own Nanny speaking and she found herself responding to it as if she were a child.

Jeannie, who had looked after her when Torquil left for Edinburgh, was a middle-aged, sweet-faced woman who had devoted her life to other people's children. First Torquil, and then Jamie, had been "her baby."

She fussed over Clola like a mother-hen, and gradually the poison had gone from Clola's body and she felt herself coming back to life as if she had been on a long, dark journey into the unknown.

"I never trusted that Mistress Forse," Jeannie said over and over again. "I sensed her wickedness even while she were wi' us but couldna' put ma finger on it."

Clola shrank from asking who had found Mrs. Forse when she had fallen from the battlements and what had happened.

It all seemed in retrospect like a horrible, evil

dream, but she could not think of how near she had been to death without shuddering.

"I saved you, didn't I?" Jamie asked her when she was well enough to talk to him. "I ran for Torquil as you told me to and he came over the roofs so quickly I couldn't keep up with him."

"Yes, you saved me, dearest," Clola agreed.

"Jeannie says I'm to look after you until Uncle Taran comes back."

"You are doing that very well," Clola said with a smile.

When Jamie had left her bed-side she had lain worrying ceaselessly as to whether Torquil would be in time and if the Duke would believe him.

She could understand how hard it would be for him to realise the violence of the hatred for the English which still possessed many of the Clansmen.

She could not help feeling frantically afraid in case he should dismiss Torquil's message as a lot of nonsense and that Euan Forse would assassinate the King.

Even if an unsuccessful attempt was made, she knew it would be a terrible blow to the pride of the McNarns, and, worse still, it would reverberate throughout the whole of Great Britain.

Living in Edinburgh amongst intelligent people, Clola had learnt how desperately the Scots were trying to establish their position.

There was intellect, invention, and industry in Scotland, ready to enrich the growth of an Imperial Britain if only the South could realise it.

But the English still behaved as if the Scots had to be kept down, and there were many unjust restrictions which affected an already impoverished economy.

Clola felt that if only there were more men of influence as well as intelligence, like the Duke, the Scottish cause could be heard and public opinion would swing in their country's favour.

But would the Duke be prepared to use his influence?

That was the real question in her mind and she wondered how she could make him understand how desperately needed he was in the Highlands.

If he would listen to the call of his blood, then there would be a chance of the Golden Age of which the Bards had sung and the Soothsayers had prophesied but which never seemed to come to fruition.

"I must talk to him," she told herself.

Then she wondered despairingly if he would listen, seeing that he had believed her to be unfaithful to him within forty-eight hours of their marriage.

How could he think such a thing? How could he believe it?

She recalled in all justice that he knew nothing about her and she was in fact at fault for not having told him of her life before she became his wife.

It all seemed to be a hopeless, imponderable problem, which kept Clola awake all night and retarded her recovery in a way which distressed and puzzled Jeannie.

Sitting now on the sofa in the Music Room, which she had made a special place of her own, Clola longed to tell the Duke not only about Scotland and his responsibilities but also about her love of music and what it meant to her.

As the evil of what had happened faded from her mind and body, she began to hear melodies carried on the breeze outside the Castle.

When she was well enough to stand at her window, looking out towards the loch, tunes came to her mind that she longed to translate into composition and song.

"If only I could explain to him," she whispered to herself, "perhaps he would . . . understand."

She remembered how they had looked into each other's eyes as she stood in front of him before she knelt for the Oath of Allegiance.

She had felt then as if they reached each other across time and there was no need for words.

Then she told herself it was just an illusion; neverthelesss, when his hands touched hers she had felt herself vibrate in a way she had never done before.

Clola was very sensitive to the vibrations of other people, and she had known at the touch of the Duke that she felt a strangeness which was spiritual.

There had also been something magic about it.

Because the thought of him disturbed her and yet at the same time she longed to see him, she started to calculate, as she had done a dozen times already, how soon he would return to the Castle.

If indeed he did return!

She had a feeling that though nothing had been said in her presence, the Duke might leave Scotland and go South with the King.

The idea hurt her so excessively that it was like a physical pain.

But she tried to tell herself it was because she was so desperately anxious to know if Euan Forse had been apprehended.

Had he been prevented from committing a ghastly murder on the instigation of his fanatical mother?

It was intended, Clola knew, that the King should sail in the *Royal George* on August 29, embarking from Port Edgar, near Kingsferry, after a visit to the Earl of Hopetoun.

Clola was sure that the Duke would stay at Hopetoun House with His Majesty, and that meant there would be no chance of his returning before August 31.

She guessed that Euan Forse would have planned to assassinate the King at the Cavalry Review on Portobello Sands.

And she felt now as if the long-drawn-out delay before she could have any news was unbearable.

Perhaps Torquil would return to tell her what had happened, and yet she doubted it! Supposing he had not been in time, or that Euan Forse had evaded them?

Bad news would not travel faster than good.

The complexity of it all made Clola so restless that, disobeying Jeannie's instructions, she rose from the sofa to walk across the room to the harp.

She had grown very much more proficient at playing the ancient instrument these past days since she had been well enough to leave her bed-room and walk, at first very unsteadily, into the other rooms of the Castle.

The day before yesterday she had been allowed to sit outside in the sunshine, warmly wrapped in one of her grandmother's beautiful sable stoles.

The feel of the sun on her face and the fresh air from the moors swept away not only the last lingering effect of Mrs. Forse's poison from Clola's body but also the terrors from her mind.

The next morning, despite Jeannie's protests when she had insisted on rising after breakfast, she had gone across the passage and entered the room of the Grey Lady.

The sunshine coming through the window dissipated the eeriness Clola had expected.

Instead, she felt that only a calm serenity pervaded the room, and looking up at the painting of the Countess Morag, she knew that the message she had received from her had in fact saved her life.

If she had not remembered that she must fight and struggle against Mrs. Forse's hold over her, she might have been too weak and too bemused by the drug to send for Torquil and to hold on to the battlements for those vital seconds before he came to save her.

Looking up at the portrait on the wall, Clola knew that she had not been mistaken on the night of her marriage when she had felt that the Grey Lady was with her.

She had been real, more real than many people she had known, and she knew that she would always be there in the future if her help was needed.

"Thank you," she said softly as she had said once before.

Then she had gone from the room with a smile on her lips and for a little while had ceased to worry about what was happening in Edinburgh.

But it was impossible to escape for long from the anxiety, which, because of her sleeplessness, was making soft purple shadows under her eyes.

She had grown much thinner during her illness and her eyes seemed larger and to fill her whole face.

But she had in fact recovered much of her strength, and she had known that that was true when yesterday she had sung, accompanying herself on the harpsichord, one of the ballads that were part of Scottish history.

Her grandmother's friends had loved to listen to her singing these ancient songs after great dinner-parties they enjoyed at her house in Edinburgh.

Because Clola knew now that only music would soothe her and prevent her from worrying over what was happening miles away, she sat down at the harp and ran her fingers over the strings.

The soft notes, she thought, were like the sound of the burn cascading down the rocks and the wash of the sea against the shore.

She plucked out note by note and now they combined to give form to the melody that had come to her mind when she was still too weak to move from her bed but knew she was safe in Jeannie's capable hands.

It was a song of the mystery of the mountains, of the wildness of the moors, and a song too . . . of love.

Clola's fingers faltered for a moment.

What did she know of love? she asked. Yet it was

there in her melody and, if she was truthful, in her heart.

A love so compelling, so inescapable, that it was no use trying to deny it.

It was the love she had sought and never found with any of the gentlemen who had asked for her hand in marriage.

She had refused them because she had known that they could never, however long she knew them, attain the ideal which lay enshrined in the secrecy of her heart.

And yet now, although tremblingly she dared not admit it, that shrine was filled.

As if the wonder of it must be translated into music, Clola played and felt the sound of it envelop her like angels' wings and lift her into the sky, from where her inspiration had come.

Then as she knew an ecstasy that came from within herself as her fingers on the strings echoed what was Divine, she was suddenly aware that she was not alone.

Something drew her compellingly and she turned her head to find, almost as if she had expected him, the Duke standing inside the door.

How long he had been there Clola had no idea; she only knew that her heart had called to him and he had answered the call.

Her hands dropped from the harp and she rose to her feet, her eyes held by the Duke's and by an expression on his face she had never seen before.

Vaguely, some part of her mind thought he looked even more handsome, more proud, and more imperious.

Then he moved slowly towards her, his eyes still holding hers, and it was impossible to think and almost impossible to breathe.

"You are all right?"

His voice, deep and low, seemed to come from another world.

"Wh-why are you . . . here so . . . soon? What has . . . happened?"

It was difficult for Clola to speak the words and there was a touch of fear behind them.

"I could not stay away any longer," the Duke replied.

Then as he stood in front of her, face to face, looking down into the mystery of her eyes, he said:

"When I first saw you, Clola, you made a vow of allegiance to me. Now I have one to make to you."

As he spoke he went down on one knee in front of her and put his hands together, palm to palm. Then, looking up to her, he said very slowly:

"I swear by Almighty God to protect and serve you for as long as my life lasts, to live or to die for you. I will love you with my whole heart, worship you as my wife, and will strive to give you happiness. May God help me!"

His voice seemed to vibrate through Clola and every word brought a response from her which seemed part of the music she had been playing.

Then because she sensed that he was waiting for her response she put her hands on each side of his.

Shyly, aware that her heart was beating wildly, she bent her head to kiss him as he had kissed her on her cheek.

But somehow instead of his cheek it was his lips she found. Then, holding her captive with his mouth, the Duke's arms were round her.

He rose to pull her close against him as his kiss deepened and became more compelling, more possessive.

Like the music which had carried Clola on angels' wings into the sky, she felt that the Duke was carrying her still higher into the heart of the spheres.

He was carrying her into a glory and a wonder that was so indescribable that she knew there were no words but only the singing of the stars.

The kiss lasted so long that they stepped out of time and only when the Duke raised his head to look down at her did Clola's hands reach out to hold on to him.

"You are mine!" the Duke said, and there was a note of triumph in his voice. "Mine, and no-one shall take you from me!"

Then he was kissing her again, kissing her fiercely, passionately, but she was not afraid.

She only knew that this was not only what she had been seeking, but what she had been made for and the reason why she had been born.

She was his, a part of him as he was a part of her, and the magic enveloping them came from other lives and other knowledge they could only find when they were together....

* * *

When Clola could speak, and it was difficult because of the wild feelings springing inside her, she asked:

"Torquil... was in... time?"

For a moment it seemed as if the Duke found it hard to think of anything but the softness of her lips. Then he answered:

"As soon as he told me what you had sent him to say, we went in search of Euan Forse. When we found him with a loaded pistol, he fired it indiscriminately in an effort to defend himself."

Clola gave a little cry of horror.

"He... might have... killed you!"

"I was not meant to die any more than you were, my precious," the Duke answered.

He held her close against him before he went on:

"I think Forse is deranged, like his mother. When we took his pistol from him he burst into an uncontrolled and violent tirade against the English."

The Duke paused for a moment before he went on:

"As far as Dunblane and I could understand, his grandparents had been killed after the Rebellion in forty-five and a cousin had her hands cut off for helping a wounded Highlander."

Clola gave a littlle murmur of horror and the Duke said gently:

"I do not want to upset you. I have left Euan Forse in the care of a competent Doctor who will see what he can do for him. We need not think of him again, any more than we need think of his mother."

Clola was still for a moment, content because the Duke's arms were round her. Then she asked:

"Why are you . . . here so soon? I was not . . . expecting you until His Majesty left Scotland."

"I told the King that I had very urgent matters to attend to at home," the Duke replied. "They were extremely urgent, because I could stay away from you no longer."

Clola raised her eyes to his and it seemed as if the sunshine was imprisoned in them.

"The King was not . . . angry with you for . . . going away?"

"He understood," the Duke answered, "but I had to promise him that I would take you South to meet him. He had heard so much of your beauty and your brilliance."

Clola blushed and the Duke asked:

"Why did you not tell me how talented you were?"

"I did not . . . think you would be . . . interested," she replied. "But there are so many . . . things I want to . . . talk to you . . . about."

"We have our whole lives in which to talk to each

other," the Duke answered "but now I only want to kiss you."

He would have sought her lips again, but Clola put up her hands.

"You must be . . . tired. I am sure you have been riding for . . . many hours."

"I rode all through the night."

"To . . . see me?" she asked incredulously.

"To see you!"

"Then you must be both tired and hungry," she said. "I am sure a bath will be waiting for you, and we will dine as soon as you are changed."

"Shall I come and help you dress, as you have no lady's-maid?" the Duke asked with a smile.

Clola blushed.

"No, of course . . . not; The housemaids will . . . help me."

"When we have finished dinner we will send them away and I will look after you as I wish to do."

Clola turned her face against his shoulder to hide her shyness. Then she gave a little laugh.

"Why do you laugh?" the Duke asked.

"My sister-in-law would be so . . . shocked," she explained. "She thinks that a man's . . . work is . . . outside and he has no . . . interest in . . . women's dress."

"I have a great interest in what you wear or do not wear," the Duke said, "and I assure you I am quite experienced in such matters."

"I can . . . believe . . . that," Clola whispered.

He smiled as he lifted her face up to his.

"Are you jealous, my darling?" he asked. "I should be very proud if I thought anything I could do would make you jealous."

She did not answer and he looked down at her face to say hoarsely:

"Could anyone be so beautiful, so perfect, so different in every way?"

His lips took hers captive and he kissed her until the room seemed to whirl round them and the Castle itself seemed to dissolve into the sunlit sky.

Then urgently, because she loved him and because she wanted the night to come so that they could be alone, Clola drew him by the hand down the passage towards their bed-rooms with their communicating-door.

* * *

Clola stirred against the Duke's shoulder and he kissed her forehead.

"You are not too tired, my darling?"

"How can I be . . . tired when I have never . . . known such . . . happiness?"

"I have really made you happy?"

She pressed her lips against his chest and he tightened his arms about her, thinking that the soft warmth of her body was the most perfect thing he had ever known.

She had not thought it possible for a man to be so passionate and yet so gentle, so demanding and yet so tender.

The Duke looked up for a moment at the great embroidered canopy overhead, just visible in the light from the one candle which still flickered behind the curtains.

"It is fate that brought you to me," he said quietly.

"That is . . . what the . . . Grey Lady said," Clola murmured.

"The Grey Lady? How do you know about her?"

There was a little pause, then Clola answered:

"If I tell you . . . you might . . . think I am very . . . foolish."

"I would think nothing you said or did was foolish. How could I when everything you have done for me, for the Clan, and for Torquil has been so wise and so completely and absolutely right?"

Clola looked up at him, and although she did not ask the question, the Duke realised what she wanted to know, and he said:

"Torquil told me, my precious, how you saved him from the MacAuads. Could anyone else have been so wonderful or so resourceful?"

Clola gave a little sigh of relief and the Duke said:

"Have you forgiven me for what I said to you? I realise now, although I was hardly aware of it at the time, that I was wildly, furiously jealous!"

"How did you . . . know I had left the . . . Castle?"

"Mrs. Forse told me."

"Mrs. . . . Forse?"

"Yes, that devillish woman through whom I might have lost you."

There was a note of fear in the Duke's voice that was unmistakable.

He turned Clola's face up to his and kissed her first on the lips, then on both her eyes, and finally once again on her lips.

Her response made the fire rise within him.

With an effort Clola moved her mouth from his.

"Go on . . . telling me about . . . Mrs. Forse," she pleaded.

"If only I had known what she was like," the Duke said, "and Dunblane blames himself for not having suspected she was insane."

"What did she . . . say to . . . you?"

"She awakened me to say: 'I'm awfu' worried, Yer Grace.'

" 'Why, what has happened?' I enquired.

" 'Her Grace left th' Castle nigh on two hours ago an' hasna returned.'

" 'Left the Castle?' I exclaimed.

"It seemed so incomprehensible that I sent the

woman away and went to your bed-room. Your nightgown was lying on the floor, the wardrobe was open, and I knew that Mrs. Forse had not lied."

"I wonder how she . . . knew I was . . . gone," Clola murmured.

"Doubtless because her bed-room overlooks the front of the house," the Duke answered. "But I was certain that you had some clandestine reason for going out at such an unearthly hour, especially after you had sent me away because Jamie was sleeping in your arms."

He paused for a moment before he said:

"Do you know how beautiful you looked with the child's head on your breast, your hair falling over your shoulders, your eyes wide and a little frightened?"

He pulled her almost roughly against him.

"My adorable little love, supposing you had died and I had never been able to make you mine as you are now?"

"But I am . . . alive," Clola whispered softly, "and I . . . love you!"

"I will make you love me more and more," the Duke promised, "only never again will there be any misunderstanding between us, nor will we ever be separated."

He kissed her forehead, then he said:

"You were telling me about the Grey Lady. I cannot imagine how you knew about her."

"Is she . . . really called the . . . 'Grey Lady'?"

"In all the legends that is how we refer to her."

"I did not . . . know that," Clola said. "But the first night when Mrs. Forse . . . cursed me and said only . . . evil would come of our . . . marriage, I was . . . afraid of her and . . . afraid of you."

"I promise that you will never feel that way again," the Duke said.

"But I knew you . . . hated the idea of . . . marrying

me! I felt it . . . when the Minister . . . joined us as . . . man and wife."

"I did not look at you then," the Duke said. "I did not dare to."

"I can understand that . . . but I felt . . . lonely and . . . afraid," Clola explained. "Then I felt that if I watched the Kilcraigs celebrating outside the Castle and . . . listened to the . . . music of the . . . pipes, I would feel . . . better."

The Duke moved his lips over the softness of her skin.

He had been right, he told himself; it had the velvet texture of a magnolia. But, though it moved him, he listened to what she was telling him.

"I went into the bed-room on the other . . . side of the . . . corridor to look out," Clola went on, "and when I was feeling . . . miserable and . . . unhappy, I knew a Grey Lady was standing beside me. She comforted me and gave me . . . courage."

"How did you know that?" he asked, then added quickly: "That is a stupid question. I know what you felt. Go on!"

"She said quite clearly," Clola continued, "that it was . . . fate that had . . . brought me here and there were . . . things for me to do which no-one else . . . could."

"She was right," the Duke said, "and I know that while you were born a Kilcraig you are now irrefutably a McNarn."

He smiled before he continued:

"The Grey Lady, Morag Countess McNarn, lost her husband in the Battle of Flodden. Forever afterwards she wore not black but grey, and she brought up her three sons to be as noble, brave, and just as their father had been. The eldest became one of the greatest Chieftains the McNarns have ever known."

He paused for a moment before he said slowly and impressively:

"Whenever the Chieftain of the Clan is in danger or in real trouble, it is understood that the Grey Lady comes to help and advise him. That she came to you, my darling, is so significant that I know now what I have to do."

"What is . . . that?" Clola asked.

"I think you know the answer," the Duke replied. "Stay here with my people, as I know you would want me to do."

Clola gave a cry of sheer happiness.

"Do you mean . . . that? Do you . . . really mean . . . it?"

"I knew when I led them in the Cavalry Review," the Duke said, "that they meant to me something impossible to ignore. I knew, when they brought me their problems, where my duty lay. And when I thought of you, I realised that my heart, which I never knew I had before, belonged to Scotland."

"Oh, my wonderful . . . magnificent husband, that is what I have . . . prayed you might . . . feel. Our country needs you so . . . desperately. There is so much to . . . do, so much to . . . fight for . . . so much to . . . live for."

Tears came to Clola's eyes with the intensity of her feelings. Then the Duke asked:

"Do you love me enough to help me? I shall need your help and your love, because I cannot live without it."

"I love you!" Clola said passionately. "With my whole . . . heart and . . . soul I am yours, completely and absolutely . . . as you know . . . I am."

"That is what I want," the Duke said. "That is what I must have, and, my darling, whatever the difficulties ahead, I know that our love will surmount them."

His lips were on hers as he spoke the last words.

Then he was kissing her with a passion and fire that seemed to come from the wildness of the moors and the spirit of the mountains.

It was, Clola knew, as beautiful as the music which throbbed within them both and made the desire of their love a rising crescendo of wonder and rapture that carried them away on the wings of ecstasy.

'I love . . . you! I love . . . you!' she thought, as her lips were held captive by his.

Their bodies were entwined, and their souls were closer still.

They had found, as few are privileged to find, the perfection of a love that belongs to the brave and valiant and those who must live as well as die for their faith.

ABOUT THE AUTHOR

BARBARA CARTLAND, the celebrated romantic novelist, historian, playwright, lecturer, political speaker, and television personality, has now written over two hundred books. She has had a number of historical books published and several biographical ones, including a biography of her brother, Major Ronald Cartland, who was the first Member of Parliament to be killed in the war. The book has a preface by Sir Winston Churchill.

In private life Barbara Cartland is a Dame of Grace of St. John of Jerusalem and one of the first women, after a thousand years, to be admitted to the Chapter General.

She has fought for better conditions and salaries for midwives and nurses, and, as President of the Hertfordshire Branch of the Royal College of Midwives, she has been invested with the first Badge of Office ever given in Great Britain, which was subscribed to by the midwives themselves.

Barbara Cartland has also championed the cause of old people and founded the first Romany Gypsy Camp in the world. It was christened "Barbaraville" by the gypsies.

Barbara Cartland is deeply interested in Vitamin Therapy and is President of the National Association for Health.